The Berenstain Bears'®

Neighbor in Need

Story and Pictures by
Jan & Mike Berenstain

HOORAY!

Sydney
& Nate devries

can read this book!

Dear Parent:
Your child's love of reading starts here!

Every child learns to read in a different way and at his or her own speed. You can help your young reader improve and become more confident by encouraging his or her own interests and abilities. You can also guide your child's spiritual development by reading stories with biblical values and Bible stories, like I Can Read! books published by Zonderkidz. From books your child reads with you to the first books he or she reads alone, there are I Can Read! books for every stage of reading:

SHARED READING
Basic language, word repetition, and whimsical illustrations, ideal for sharing with your emergent reader.

BEGINNING READING
Short sentences, familiar words, and simple concepts for children eager to read on their own.

READING WITH HELP
Engaging stories, longer sentences, and language play for developing readers.

READING ALONE
Complex plots, challenging vocabulary, and high-interest topics for the independent reader.

ADVANCED READING
Short paragraphs, chapters, and exciting themes for the perfect bridge to chapter books.

I Can Read! books have introduced children to the joy of reading since 1957. Featuring award-winning authors and illustrators and a fabulous cast of beloved characters, I Can Read! books set the standard for beginning readers.

A lifetime of discovery begins with the magical words **"I Can Read!"**

Visit www.icanread.com for information on enriching your child's reading experience.
Visit www.zonderkidz.com for more Zonderkidz I Can Read! titles.

"In the same way, let your light shine before men, that they may see your good deeds and praise your Father in heaven."
—Matthew 5:16

ZONDERKIDZ

The Berenstain Bears'™ Neighbor in Need

Requests for information should be addressed to:
Zonderkidz, *Grand Rapids, Michigan 49530*

Library of Congress Cataloging-in-Publication Data

Berenstain, Jan, 1923-
The Berenstain Bears' neighbor in need / written by Jan and Mike Berenstain.
p. cm. — (I can read. Level 1)
ISBN 978-0310-72098-0 (softcover)
[1. Helpfulness—Fiction. 2. Bears—Fiction. 3. Christian life—Fiction. I. Berenstain, Michael. II. The Berenstain Bears' Neighbor in need. III. Neighbor in need
PZ7. B44826Bin 2011
[E]—dc 2010016486

Editor: Mary Hassinger

Printed in China
10 11 12 13 14 15 /SCC/ 10 9 8 7 6 5 4 3 2 1

The Berenstain Bears'® Neighbor in Need

Story and Pictures By

Jan and Mike Berenstain

“The Good Deed Scouts
are on the job!” said Scout Sister.
“We do a good deed each and every day,”
said Scout Lizzy.

"As the Bible says," Scout Fred pointed out, "we should be 'rich in good deeds.'"

"Good point, Fred," said Scout Brother.

"Look," said Sister.

"Mrs. Grizzle is mowing grass.

That looks hard!"

Mrs. Grizzle was the cubs' babysitter.

"Hello, Mrs. Grizzle," said Brother.

"May we help you?"

"Thanks!" said Mrs. Grizzle.

"Be my guest! This is hot work.

I will get us all a cool drink."

The Good Deed Scouts pushed
the lawn mower.

They pulled dandelions.

They weeded the flower beds.

They trimmed bushes.

They got hot and tired.

Mrs. Grizzle came out with

a tray of lemonade.

They all sat down in the shade to cool off. The lemonade tasted great.

"Do you need more help, Mrs. Grizzle?" asked Sister.

"Do I ever!" laughed Mrs. Grizzle. "There's always work to be done around here!"

The Good Deed Scouts took out the garbage.

They swept the garage.

The Good Deed Scouts walked
Mrs. Grizzle's dog, Scooter.
They gave her cat, Daisy, a bath.

Daisy did not like her bath.
She climbed up the
kitchen curtains!

Mrs. Grizzle helped the Scouts dry off.

"You Scouts worked very hard,"

said Mrs. Grizzle.

"You should get something back."

"We don't want anything," said Brother.

“Good Deed Scouts do a good deed
each and every day.
Like it says in the Book of Matthew:
‘In everything, do to others
what you would want them to do to you.’”

“That’s fine,” Mrs. Grizzle said.

“But I do good deeds too.

I like to do tricks.

Would you like to see some?”

“Oh, yes!” said the Scouts.

The cubs loved her amazing tricks.

So Mrs. Grizzle
did tricks.
She pulled a
rabbit out of
a hat.

She made
a bunch of
flowers appear
out of the air.

She pulled a quarter out of Lizzy's ear.

For her last trick, Mrs. Grizzle took Fred's scarf and folded it. When she unfolded it, a dove flew out! The Good Deed Scouts clapped and cheered.

G
G
GOOD
GOOD
DEED

But Mrs. Grizzle wasn't finished.
She got out her banjo and flute.
"Now I will play 'Dixie'
and 'Yankee Doodle' at the same time."

And she did too!
The scouts clapped
and cheered more.

It was time for the Scouts to go home.

“Just a minute,” said Mrs. Grizzle.

She cut three bunches of flowers
from her garden.
She gave the flowers to the Scouts.
"These are for your mothers," she said.
"Thank you, Mrs. Grizzle!"
said the Scouts, waving goodbye.

Scouts Brother and Sister gave
their flowers to Mama Bear.
"Oh, they're so pretty!" said Mama.
She put them in water
and set them on the table.

"Nice flowers!" said Papa Bear
at dinner.
"Mrs. Grizzle gave them to us,"
said Sister.
"That Mrs. Grizzle
is so thoughtful," said Papa.

"And so are our very own
Good Deed Scouts!" said Mama Bear.
"The Lord blesses anyone
who does good!"

Designing Intelligent Systems

An Introduction

Designing Intelligent Systems

An Introduction

Igor Aleksander

New York

First published in Great Britain by
Kogan Page, London. This edition published in
the United States by UNIPUB

ISBN 0-89059-043-5

Library of Congress Catalog Card Number
84-40552

Printed and bound in Great Britain

Contents

Preface

This book is based on a series of lectures delivered as part of a multi-disciplinary course to a class of first-year undergraduate students at Brunel University, England. The students were attending courses in electrical engineering, psychology and information systems management.

The nature of the course was challenging because it introduced a novel and ill-defined subject to students with virtually no knowledge of the underpinning topics: mathematics and computing. Consequently, the book is aimed at a very broad readership and truly represents an introduction to this new and absorbing subject. But perhaps the book also aims to achieve a little more than this. Being basic in approach, it has been necessary to include in it only those concepts that are truly fundamental. As the subject in itself is still very much in its infancy, this has meant concentrating on issues that are largely independent of technological 'nuts and bolts'. After much sifting, these fundamentals appeared to centre on systems that help to clarify vague ideas and so allow us to begin to understand the sense in which a system might be said to be 'intelligent'.

Modelling techniques were the next fundamental issue to be considered, and here aspects of automata theory and mathematics have been chosen as foundation topics. The nature of computer programs is clearly central to the design of intelligent systems, so that some well-known programming schemes in this area have been included.

Two chapters on current applications have been included so as not to leave the reader with the impression that the subject is purely theoretical. Finally, there is a glimpse into a possible future, and a description of a possible algorithm that would 'get to know' its user.

Introduction

Intelligent systems as a cornerstone of information technology

We live in an era in which extraordinary claims are being made about the achievements of computers. Every few days the media report on some new super-intelligent feat that someone in an artificial intelligence laboratory somewhere has made. Yet another Grand Master at chess might have been defeated by a machine, or a computer might, without human intervention, have composed a new symphony that sounds just like Beethoven. One even hears of programs that are likely to do away with the human general practitioner.

Unfortunately, when examined closely, such systems only create an *illusion* of intelligence. Computers work very fast, and it is this speed that lies at the heart of the illusion. The all-powerful chess-playing machines of today are really no better than that built by Johann Nepomuk Maelzel in 1830. This machine thrilled audiences by beating its human challengers at chess until it was exposed (by Edgar Allan Poe, among others) as a fake. There was a man hidden inside it! The man hidden inside the modern chess-playing machine is the programmer. He has simply stored some good chess-playing principles, and offset the lack of flexibility of such a set by finding fast ways for the machine to look a long way ahead.

Fortunately, these illusions are being recognized as such and a new science of intelligent systems design is beginning to take shape. The ultimate aim of this science is to create machines in which intelligence is measured not by the way it outsmarts human users, but by the excellence with which it meets human needs. If there is any value to what is known as *advanced information technology* (or *informatics*), it will be to spread the benefits of computing power to ever widening populations.

Breaking away from programming: the task for intelligent systems

The ultimate line of attack is the machine that makes no demands of its user so far as programming is concerned. Clearly, such a machine will have to see, hear and understand. To do this it will need to spend some time in negotiating the meaning of the every-day things in life, so as to provide a bedrock of knowledge on which to build. This will have to be an on-going process, as the machine and its user must continually be updating their knowledge of each other. This book is about the sort of design principles that need to be understood if such systems are ever to be brought to fruition.

Artificial intelligence is a branch of computer science which clearly demonstrates that computers are capable of tackling logical as well as numerical problems. It is not the intention of this book to provide a manual of artificial intelligence, but parts of the book do introduce artificial intelligence techniques and expert systems. The latter are examples of practical applications of artificial intelligence which enable a computer-user to interact with a machine that contains a large collection of facts and rules. The perspective of this book is such that it considers artificial intelligence as being just one component among many that are being used in the quest to provide the machine that learns about its user, and that makes its computing power available without demanding that the user should learn a set of programming techniques.

An overview of the book

Clearly, no intelligent system of the kind outlined above exists in practice. Therefore, it is not possible to take a descriptive approach in discussing systems design. Rather, this book is directed at resolving an ideal intelligent system into its potential elements. It is believed that these elements now exist in computer science, electronics and mathematics.

AN INTRODUCTION TO SYSTEMS

Close examination has been made of the meaning of words, so that the potential for misunderstanding, even when dealing with key terms such as *intelligent* and *system,* is reduced. This definitional attitude is the subject of Chapter 1. After a brief look at previous attempts at defining *systems theory* as a body of knowledge that provides unification, the opposite view is taken: that systems design must involve an appreciation of a variety of non-overlapping methods and theories that have a potential for contributing to the target design. A system is seen as a way of isolating an element of the world so as to be able to study it without interference from other elements. The chapter introduces a systematic way of measuring the attributes of systems by a framework of constructs (such as *manufactured* and *natural*).

The chapter ends with a discussion of a novel construct: *intentionality* and the lack thereof. This is very much a human construct and deals with our ability to relate to other people and objects, by understanding inwardly their likely behaviour. This is thought to be the key construct that will distinguish between illusory and real intelligent systems.

AUTOMATA THEORY

The subject for Chapter 2 is quite specific in that it introduces automata theory, the modelling technique used for dealing with systems having inner complexity. There is no doubt that intelligent systems have considerable inner complexity, which this approach helps to simplify. The power of automata (used in the formal sense) is that they provide a graphical way of visualizing this inner complexity and, indeed, of being able to construct diagrams to illustrate a large variety of inner modes of behaviour. A further pointer to the fundamental nature of formal automata is that there exist totally mechanical ways of turning the graphical representation (known as a *state structure*) into either hardware or software. This means that a system may be designed in the first instance without having to take into consideration such details as the language in which the programs will be written, or the type of chips that will be used in the hardware. After considering a design example at this abstract level, the modelling power of automata is broached again by means of two very different examples. The first is couched in terms of a game of cards played by three people using three strategies. It illustrates the potential of the model not necessarily for card games only, but also for similar situations that could occur in business management, stock markets and strategic studies. The second example is related to psychological modelling where an automaton model is used to provide an explanation of dreaming. This is typical of a class of modelling problems, highly pertinent to intelligent systems, for which only vague theories exist within psychology.

MATHEMATICAL MODELLING

The mathematical basis for informational systems is quite different from that of more classical branches of engineering and physics. In a curious way, the division neatly coincides with another division in mathematics itself: classical and modern. Classical mathematics more or less ended at the turn of the century, although the rumblings of modern theories go back more than two hundred years. It is not so much the subject matter that has changed between the old and the new, as the way in which the *use* of mathematics has been reconstrued. Chapter 3 starts with a review of these changes and shows that modern mathematics is more about logical deductions from a set of *abstract* facts than about predictions of events in the real world. Although this sounds rather devoid of purpose it bears a strong affinity with the operations carried out by any informational machine, whether it be an abstract automaton or a computer program. The logical steps that are found in mathematics between axioms and theorems are analogous to the logical steps taken by an informational system during the course of its operation. In Chapter 3 there are examples of the properties that are looked for in modern mathematical systems, and the way in which these may affect information system models is discussed. In particular, the semi-group is considered: this is the mathematical twin of the finite state automaton discussed in Chapter 2.

ARTIFICIAL INTELLIGENCE

At this point the book turns its attention to the word *intelligent.* Probably the only technical use made of that word previously was in artificial intelligence. This is introduced in Chapter 4 which draws attention to an alternative form of modelling to the automata described in Chapter 2. The word 'algorithm' is a synonym to 'recipe', so the algorithmic models described here are recipes that achieve some stated aim. The aim in artificial intelligence is to perform tasks on a computer which, if done by humans, would be said to require intelligence. Typical are programs that play games, solve problems, and begin to get to grips with the extraction of meaning from simple sentences input into a computer in natural language. Scientists researching artificial intelligence have, as far as possible, tried to make their work independent of the details of the machine on which their programs run or of the particular computer language they use. In this sense the algorithms presented become automata of specific kinds, and departures from classical automata add interest to this work.

USE OF INTELLIGENT SYSTEMS

In the 1960s the major expectations for artificial intelligence were in the fields of automation and space exploration. Making robots more intelligent was the object of much work in the field of automation, while for the space programme the creation of exploration machines with on-board intelligence was the standard objective. In fact, neither of these aims have yet been achieved, the latter for political reasons in the sense that expenditure on space exploration was drastically reduced in the USA in the 1970s, while the former faltered for technical reasons. It is still likely that one of the major outlets for pragmatic intelligent systems will be the factory floor. In Chapter 5 some of the gaps between the needs required for automatic production and the solutions offered by artificial intelligence come under scrutiny. Central to this argument is the impact of the industrial robot. While intelligent information processing has grown away from industrial problems, the mechanical aspects of robots have developed along much more practical lines. For instance, mechanical manipulator arms, driven by simple repetitive programs lodged in largely non-intelligent computers, are now commonplace.

EXPERT SYSTEMS

Probably the most successful application of artificial intelligence in the commercial sense is the expert system. This is almost a direct spin-off of classical work in artificial intelligence and cashes in on techniques for making logical deductions by means of a program. The logical relationships pertaining to a particular area of expertise (such as the diagnosis of disease from a set of symptoms) are fed into the machine by an expert. Such information can subsequently be used by non-experts who interrogate the machine in near-natural language. This technique is examined in Chapter 6 and some of the more successful applications are presented as case studies. Attention is also drawn to the limitations of expert system methods, as this provides important pointers to possible future research trends.

A LOOK FORWARD

It seems important that attempts are made to break away from some of the limitations of artificial intelligence. In Chapter 7 the accent is shifted from the coldly logical action of a computer model of stored knowledge to a situation where programs and systems begin to develop a better understanding of their users. This simultaneously affords to the user a better understanding of the machine with which he is interacting. After all, the ultimate mark of a truly intelligent machine may be in its ability to understand. This implies the use of methods that can cope with the fuzziness of the real world and are able to create idealized representations of such fuzzy data. This field is currently being researched and contains many unsolved problems. An introduction is made to one particular approach in such research and this is related to the possible changes that may be expected in artificial intelligence in the future.

This book then is directed towards those who are embarking on courses of study or self-education in the emerging field of information technology. No prior knowledge of computers, engineering or mathematics is required. An agile and open mind will suffice. Looking towards the next century, those who are new to the field now will experience the most enormous changes in engineering techniques, and these will both impinge on and guide the evolution of intelligent systems. The central aim of the book is to try to anticipate those design principles that might provide a framework for this rapidly advancing process of technical invention.

CHAPTER 1

What is a system and how can it be intelligent?

Historical notions

It may seem excessively pedantic to question the meaning of simple words, when it is clear that the target for discussion is specific. The trouble is that use of the word *system* evokes a wide variety of notions depending on who is using it and who is hearing it. One of the central points of this book is that the design of intelligent systems is a multi-disciplinary process. The designer of an intelligent system will have to keep a very clear head about his procedures. He will need to take notice of systems in industry, as well as those that occur in nature. Further, he will have to understand the interfaces between human and mechanical systems.

Engineers and scientists are very fond of using the word system. They often extol the virtues of the 'systems approach'. What is generally meant is that a methodical approach is being used. It has also been competently argued that there are surprising similarities between ways in which totally different systems operate. The eminent biologist Ludwig von Bertalanffy (1973) probably coined the phrase *general system theory* and published an important book on the subject. The core of this theory is that there exists a body of tools (mainly mathematical) that may be applied in a variety of seemingly disconnected fields. For example, topography (the mathematical way of specifying the way in which things are connected) finds application both in the design of transportation systems and the design of electronic networks.

Although this book does not shy away from looking for such similarities, it tries not to lose sight of the alternative point of view, that the *differences* between different kinds of systems are vitally important too. If one accepts that at least one role for an intelligent system will be to provide a better match between man and machine, its designer must be fully aware of the differences between these two systems.

Systems: a way of partitioning complex worlds

It is often a good thing if the technologist can choose his words so as to have a meaning close to its colloquial meaning. What then does the dictionary make of the word 'system'? There are several definitions, ranging from the tangible to the abstract.

At the most tangible level there is:

> 'Anything made of parts placed together or adjusted into a regular, connected whole.';

while at the most abstract level:

> 'A full and connected view of some department of knowledge.'

Worth noting in these definitions are the words 'together' and 'connected'. The feeling is one of parts interconnecting to achieve some specific purpose. There is an implied cohesiveness among these parts, with a much looser connection to the rest of the world.

A good way of intensifying this understanding is to test it with some specific examples. Take a motor car engine, for example, this has all the markings of a system. Even though a connection is required via the drive shaft to the rest of the car, there is a far tighter coupling between its own internal parts. Now take a book; even though it has the appearance of a system, in the sense that the pages are the parts and the binding provides the togetherness, we feel uneasy to dub a book in this way. The feeling of unease stems from the fact that the pages are really not interacting in a functional way, the binding being there for the convenience of merely grouping *parts of a whole* together. So in some sense a book is a system, but we note the need for expressing its functional complexity in some way.

A further complication about a book is that its contents may well be a substantial system under the second dictionary definition. We shall return to this 'inner' and 'outer' character of functional things often in this book. For now, suffice it to say that it is often the case in systems that 'use' information, that the outer part forms a physical system, whilst the inner part uses an informational one. These two systems are totally different in kind, and yet are intimately coupled to one another. A typical example of such a system is the digital computer; this has circuits intimately interconnected to form a system (the hardware), while the associated software program is a totally different informational system of interconnected instructions and computer-language statements. And yet, to achieve the purpose of the program it is essential that these systems work in perfect unison.

Take now what is probably one of the most complex of systems: the human being. Not only does the inner/outer connection hold (philosophers call it the *body/mind problem*), but there are also several other systems required to keep the whole human functioning. These are chemical (eg digestion), hydraulic (eg blood flow) and, indeed, there are many others on which the reader may wish to speculate.

All this suggests an important point about systems. They help to determine ways in which the things of the world are categorized. The point is that not only does this division occur at the level of physical space, but also at levels of function that require a considerable degree of abstraction to understand them. For example, it may be quite possible for a neurophysiologist to plot out the exact physical connections of cells in the brain, but unless he knows about the history and experience of the particular brain he is considering he cannot predict or even ponder on the likely way in which the human owning that brain is likely, for example, to answer questions about which is his favourite dessert. This is what we mean by abstraction. To predict informational behaviour of the dessert kind, the predictor must know something less observable than cells: the likes and dislikes of the owner of that brain.

There are cases where the inner system may be studied almost independently. This is particularly true of computer programs. A chess-playing program, for example, may be studied as an entity apart from the hardware of the computer on which it will run. Indeed, a very important question that will be raised later in this book is whether, having studied a chess-playing computer program to some depth, the system is valid both in the context of a machine and a human being.

The conclusion reached is that the word 'system', outside of its important role of categorizing things, should not be assumed to have a hard and fast technical meaning. What is important, if one is bent on defining things, is the attribute of the word that is usually placed before the word 'system'. In heading towards such an attribute (*intelligent* system) some other attributes will be considered in order to see if they help to clarify matters.

The trivial/non-trivial construct

A construct can be defined as a double-pole notion. The two poles (trivial and non-trivial in this case) can be imagined to be the limits of a scale against which a particular kind of system may be measured. This technique is sometimes called the *repertory grid* method (see Bannister & Fransella, 1971), developed from the work of Kelly (1955) on the *theory of personal constructs.* Given this scale, we can attempt to place some systems on it. Take a 'dangly earring', for instance, it qualifies as a system as it is made up of connected parts working together, but it holds very little interest for someone who likes to find out how things work. Therefore, choosing which of the above poles is the more appropriate one would probably decide on the trivial pole. On the other hand, a chess-playing program, because its operation is not obvious and may be quite interesting, would be towards the non-trivial pole. The measurement of elements against constructs acts not only as a categorizing tool within the class of systems (in this case), but also points to similarities between constructs which help to clarify the meaning of the constructs themselves. For example, here we have identified the similarity between the trivial/non-trivial construct and the interesting/not interesting one.

But beware! The word 'personal' in Kelly's theory draws attention to the fact that different people may classify elements in different ways. For example, to a fashion designer, a dangly earring may be anything but trivial.

The manufactured/natural construct

There is quite a clear boundary here, because things are either manufactured or natural. There is probably much less dispute about this than more abstract constructs. By being interested in the design of intelligent systems we are aiming to straddle both sides of the construct.

The intelligent/non-intelligent construct

Finally, we arrive at the central construct in this book with the aim of trying to outline our interest in systems we may call 'intelligent'. The word is associated with endless ambiguities, some of which are controversial. For example, if we are to compare men and machines, some may make statements such as: 'Machines cannot be intelligent because they do not partake in the social process of interacting with intelligent humans.' This implies that the intelligent/non-intelligent split occurs at the natural/manufactured division. It also implies that, when compared with humans, machines can never be seen as being intelligent in the same way. At the same time, one hears chess-playing programs described as being 'intelligent'. This seems a fair description, as some such programs have been known to beat chess masters who, by most definitions, may be regarded as being intelligent.

Even more pertinent is the fact that there are many forces among humans which lead them to divide other humans into intelligent and non-intelligent classes. Not only is this common throughout educational systems, but also an individual may be IQ-tested and classified accordingly, or may be classified by the mental health services, in addition to the continuous judgements that are made on him as he progresses through the educational system. The construct is undoubtedly fuzzy, and one can justifiably question whether it is right to dub a technological area, as that of intelligent systems is intended to be, with this lack of precision.

It has been mentioned earlier that this has been done in the field of artificial intelligence. This, however, turns out to be a good example of the way in which the word 'intelligence' has brought about a degree of confusion. The most widely accepted definition of artificial intelligence is 'doing on computers that which, if done by humans, would be called intelligent'. This merely imports the difficulty of using the word, in the human sense, in a technological sense. Indeed, artificial intelligence does not define a common interest among its supporters. Some claim it to be the ultimate theory of *human* behaviour, while others, more soberly, see it as a collection of clever programming techniques. We shall return to this debate in other parts of this book – here we wish only to suggest a rapid way in which the concept of an intelligent system may be made clearer.

The intentional/non-intentional construct

In the presence of the ever-increasing number of expert systems which, for example, may be capable of giving medical advice, a particular question becomes pertinent. What is the basic distinction between the kind of intelligence displayed by a medical advice-giving program, and that of an advice-giving doctor? It makes sense to assume that the question needs, at least, to be approached, even if it might be difficult to find a totally satisfactory answer. It would certainly be wrong to pretend that the machinery whose design principles are to be discussed later in this book, can be called 'intelligent' in the same way as a human being as soon as it pronounces human-like sentences.

Simply, the issue may be brought into focus by imagining a human listener's reaction on hearing first a computer and then a human doctor pronounce: 'I know what you mean when you say that your headache is unbearable ...' Were the listener even the most avid *aficionado* of computing, he would find it hard to believe the computer. He would need to imagine a situation in which the computer has actually experienced a headache. It is the role of experience in the make up of the intelligence of a human being that creates the greatest distinction between artificial and natural systems. In philosophy, this notion of the relationship between human mental events and experience of the real world is called *intentionality.* The concept was first developed by Franz Brentano, a German philosopher, in 1874. The precise meaning of the word is somewhat different from its everyday, general meaning. In philosophy it is used to point to the property of 'knowing what one is talking about' when referring to objects in the real world.

If I hear someone using the word 'bacon', this conjures up in my head an entire collection of memories: the look of a slice of bacon, the smell of it, as well as its taste and feel. But central to the concept is not only this set of memories, but also how they got there. In other words, the reason that I know about bacon is not because I read about it in a book, or because someone taught me its smell, taste, etc, but because at some time I must have eaten some as a result of being hungry. At that time I must have decided whether I liked it or not and whether to repeat the experience or otherwise. It is this knowledge that comes from an involvement with the object that is called *intentionality.*

We shall see later in this book that in the world of artificial intelligence, computer programs have been developed that begin to cope with input submitted in natural language. Both story-writing and story-understanding programs have been written. The latter appear to perform in a manner similar to that of a young child who is set a comprehension test after having been told a story. For example, a computer, having been given the story of *Little Miss Muffet,* and being asked the question: 'Why was Miss Muffet frightened?', might well calculate the answer: 'Because a spider frightened her.' On the other hand, a child might answer: 'Because spiders wiggle and tickle and move very fast.'

We shall also see later in this book that a major development in artificial intelligence has been the *expert system.* Such a program builds on the ability of a computer to manipulate natural language in the following way. It can communicate with an expert in some field and ask a barrage of questions. Typical areas in which this has been done are medical diagnosis and oil prospecting. The computer builds the data obtained during the interrogation into its memory, which can subsequently be used by a lesser expert. Not only can he retrieve relevant answers to questions, but also he can ask the system to output the line of reasoning that led it to its answers.

Clearly an expert system could not answer in the style of the child above. What is missing in its database is the experience of actually having been frightened by a spider.

For some years now, a major philosophical debate has been raging among scientists involved in artificial intelligence on the question of whether current machines and programs, particularly those that process natural language, may be said to possess intentionality. The major proponent of the notion that no currently built machine or program has intentionality is American philosopher John Searle. He makes his point by showing that the language-handling routines in a language-understanding program are clearly just rules for handling *symbols.* He argues that a group of English-speaking people, given perfect and copious memory facilities, could be given a mass of rules relating to the manipulation of Chinese symbols. Armed with this, he argues, they are in the same position as a language-understanding computer, and would have as much success in answering questions submitted in sequences of Chinese symbols as the machine. However, no matter how successfully the job is performed, the performers of the task have no idea of the content of the story. The 'understanding' is at best partial, and at worst a mere illusion.

It needs to be said straight away that the argument put forward by Searle (1980) does not debar machines from being intentional just because they are manufactured, as opposed to natural. The argument merely points to the fact that current programming techniques have only got as far as to deal with very simple symbolic representations of real worlds. One of the intentions of this book is to show that, given a degree of sophistication in the way machines may be made to associate their own symbols with those in the real world, building systems possessing intentionality may well be a realistic goal.

The process of creating this sophistication should, even at this stage, not seem excessively mysterious. The secret lies in creating in the machine a need to resolve ambiguities that result in the real-world data that it is asked to assimilate. As an example, consider once more the story of Miss Muffet: interaction with the intentional machine might proceed as follows. When the machine is asked why Miss Muffet might have been frightened it could answer: 'The story says that it was on account of the spider. Even though I have been fed masses of data on spiders by the spider expert, *I* do not know what it's like to be frightened, or why a spider should be frightening.'

This interaction should cause the user to think of ways in which it could indicate to the machine what it's like to be frightened. Here we are beginning to anticipate the contents of a later chapter. Suffice it to say that the user would relate 'fright' to some inner operation that the computer would find 'unpleasant' in relative terms. At this point it is really hard to imagine such an interaction, so we leave the subject there for the time being.

Evidence of intentionality

American philosopher Daniel Dennett (1978) believes that one could ascribe intentionality to many of the products of current work in artificial intelligence. Indeed, he may be seen as being John Searle's major philosophical opponent. His argument starts with the simple notion that intentionality is a concept that falls into the class of beliefs. It is not measurable in quantifiable terms. Therefore, if I believe that a machine possesses intentionality, this belief could be based on a need to have such a belief rather than on clear-cut physical evidence.

Dennett uses the example of a chess-playing program. He points to the fact that an explanation of how something works can rest on three principles. The first of these is the notion of co-operative function, where one tries to explain the whole from a description of the function of its parts. For example, one might explain how a mousetrap works by reference to a sprung frame, held cocked by a catch, which is connected through a pivoted strut to a piece of cheese.

A second mode of explanation may rest on a reference to commonly known and accepted physical or chemical laws. For example, the action of a pendulum may be deduced by putting physical constants (eg length of pendulum) into a mathematical statement of Newton's laws of motion. This results in a prediction of effects such as the frequency of oscillation of the pendulum and the decrease in the range of the swing with time.

The third method is one of analogy: one thing is *like* another. This is very common when one first encounters electrical circuits and 'current down a wire' is likened to 'water down a pipe' explaining why the higher the voltage (pressure) the greater the flow (current). Since a pipe offers a 'resistance' to flow, a piece of wire is said to have 'resistance' to current.

Dennett asks us to use an explanational method on the following situation involving a human playing chess against a computer. The machine has just played and the human opponent needs to think of what the machine has just done. Were he to use the first, or functional method, he might say to himself: 'The microprocessor has entered loop 3.7HS of the third branch of its evaluation routine, and therefore I must move my Queen.' This has an obviously non-sensical ring to it. Were he to base his explanation on physical laws he might conclude that in order to win he might consider pouring a bucket of water over the circuits of the machine. Again, this seems like a less than helpful approach.

Dennett argues that the most appropriate explanation, at

least the one that is most likely to lead to a continuation of the game, is for the human player to think: 'The machine is threatening my Queen.' This is a blatant attribution of intentionality to the machine. It is also clear that it arises from the human player's *need* to believe that the machine is trying to win in the same way as a human opponent would.

This is a very similar argument to the one that British mathematician Alan Turing used in the very early days after the invention and construction of the first automatic digital computer. Turing proposed a test which would assess a machine as to whether it was intelligent or not. He invented a complicated game that would be played between three people, a man, a woman and an interrogator. They would be connected by a teletypewriter network and the object of the interrogator was to discover which of the other two was the man and which the woman. The two mystery people would be addressed as A and B, A being assigned the task of misleading the interrogator and B of helping him. This information, too, was not known by the interrogator. An interrogator, after playing the game for some time and against many pairs, would achieve a particular score of correct identifications.

Turing put the hypothesis that if one of the mystery persons were to be replaced by a machine, and that were not to alter the interrogator's average scoring rate, then that machine might be called intelligent, and according to Turing, indistinguishable from humans. Of course, Turing did not imply that such machines were available or, indeed, even possible. The Turing test effectively says that if a human is prepared to attribute human qualities to an object, then he endows it with those qualities.

These arguments tend to be torpedoed by the possibility that intelligence and intentionality may not be qualities that are amenable to testing by outward tests. We shall see in Chapter 2 that some quite simple machines can have important inner properties that never come to the fore, but are most useful in helping such devices to improve their performance. But perhaps one of the most vivid illustrations of the dangers of attribution may be found in a program written by Ed Weizenbaum of the Massachusetts Institute of Technology (1966). This program (largely designed to disprove Turing's notion of attribution) simply bounced some of its user's conversation back at him. The program is called ELIZA, and pretends to be a psychiatrist. A conversation with ELIZA might have proceeded like this:

ELIZA:	'Welcome to the surgery, what can I do for you?'
PATIENT:	'I need help, I feel awfully depressed.'
ELIZA:	'I am sorry to hear that, what depresses you?'
PATIENT:	'It's my husband, he goes out with other women.'
ELIZA:	'Tell me more about your husband.'
PATIENT:	'I've told you, he's OK but he goes out with other women!'
ELIZA:	'It may be relevant for us to talk about your parents.'
PATIENT:	'OK, if you think so.'
ELIZA:	'How do you get on with your father?'
PATIENT:	'He is dead.'
ELIZA:	'I'm sorry to hear that, tell me more.'
	⋮
PATIENT:	'I don't like my mother at all, can we get back to my husband please?'
ELIZA:	'I'm sorry to hear that. I'm afraid that we must stop now as we have run out of time.

Despite the fact that there is something extraordinarily human about the way that the program is handling the questions, Weizenbaum points to the simplicity of the scheme to dispel any notion of understanding, intentionality or intelligence in the program. It operates using two simple principles. First it stores a vast list of responses, triggered off by sets of words that might appear in the patient's discourse. Second, it is capable of structuring sentences using simple grammatical rules, and incorporating in these sentences some of the keywords used by the patient corrected for case and tense. For example, in the third line, ELIZA picks the first phrase from a list triggered by the words 'help' and 'depressed', while in the second it merely replays the word back to the patient, corrected for case. If, in the patient's first sentence the word 'distressed' had been used instead of 'depressed', ELIZA's phrase would have been: '..., what distresses you?'

In the patient's second line, ELIZA could not find responses in its database to cope with 'goes out with other women', so it chose to pick on the word 'husband' instead, leading to the patient's irritated reply. Because the patient continued on about 'women' in the next line, ELIZA used an escape route and changed the subject to 'parents'. The time termination is exercized quite early in the program, leaving most of the patient's points totally unattended. Despite this, many who encountered ELIZA attributed human properties of understanding, and even interest, to the totally 'stupid' computer program.

So, the quest for intelligent and intentional machines cannot rest with the attribution argument as used by Dennett. The crucial issue in assigning any form of human wisdom to a machine is that we must be able to understand plainly how this wisdom gets into the machine in the first place. Therefore, the design of intelligent systems must be based on a study of machines that somehow acquire knowledge, and not just of machines that use knowledge at a superficially competent level. It is the acquisition process itself that is just as important in the proper structuring of the system, as the mechanisms for using it.

Other problems in the foundation of intelligent systems

The concern that has been shown so far for finding a fundamental way of distinguishing between human and artificial intelligence has touched on topics that will be taken to a greater depth in Chapters 4 and 6. But there are other teasing questions in this field which are thought to be fundamental to the design of intelligent systems. They will be introduced only briefly here and expanded later on.

MODELLING INTELLIGENT SYSTEMS: COPING WITH DISCONTINUITY

The digital computer is one among many engineering structures that may act as hosts for systems that may be said to be 'intelligent'. Some of these will be encountered in Chapters 5 and 7, either as novel engineering structures or just as ideas that could be implemented either as novel structures or simulated on conventional computers. However, the subject is still in its infancy so that the most valuable implementations have probably yet to be invented. Therefore, a most important question is whether there exists a common theoretical background from which these systems, even the unknown ones, can be analysed. It will be seen in Chapter 2 that this analysis is likely to stem from a mathematical subject known as *automata theory.** Here we shall take a brief look at the

* Those with some knowledge of Boolean logic and automata theory may wish to skip this introductory material and go on to Chapter 2.

nature of this type of mathematics and the way in which it differs from the continuous type of mathematics that may be more familiar to students of physics or engineering.

A simple example might help at this stage. An alarm system on a steam engine is required in a situation in which the following rough measurements are taken:

pressure – high or low,
temperature – high or low,
load – high or low.

The alarm is to sound for the combinations of conditions of these measurements represented by the three vertical columns below:

	alarm conditions		
pressure (p)	high	low	low
temperature (t)	high	high	high
load (l)	high	high	low

In classical applied mathematics, models often have to assume some form of continuity. Therefore, it may be conventional to assign a meaning to 'high' and 'low' as (say) scores of 10 and 0 on a 0 – 10 scale. It may be assumed that the three variables are given the obvious symbols p, t and l, each of which can assume values in the 0 – 10 range. A linear equation might be formulated in which the variable *a* is calculated as a function of the variables:

$$a = \mathrm{p}C_{\mathrm{p}} + \mathrm{t}C_{\mathrm{t}} + \mathrm{l}C_{1}$$

where C_{p}, C_{t} and C_{1} are constant coefficients. The design of a mathematical model consists of determining values for these coefficients so that *a* is high (say 10) for the combinations of variables that require the alarm to sound. Such values may be determined by solving the following simultaneous equations:

$$\begin{aligned} 10 &= 10.C_{\mathrm{p}} + 10.C_{\mathrm{t}} + 10.C_{1} \\ 10 &= 0.C_{\mathrm{p}} + 10.C_{\mathrm{t}} + 10.C_{1} \\ 10 &= 0.C_{\mathrm{p}} + 10.C_{\mathrm{t}} + 0.C_{1} \end{aligned}$$

These equations have a single solution:

$$C_{\mathrm{t}} = 10, C_{\mathrm{p}} = 0, C_{1} = 0$$

The difficulty with this is that the alarm will sound whenever $C_{\mathrm{t}} = 10$ and the pattern high pressure, high temperature and low load is not a combination that should set off the alarm. In fact, a considerably more elaborate form of linear equation is required to distinguish between alarm and non-alarm combinations of the measured variables. However, this is not the central point at the moment. Rather, the crux of the argument is that linear mathematics is an inappropriate medium with which to model the 'intelligence' of this somewhat trivial task.

The appropriate medium for the desired model is a statement in *logical* terms rather than the *linear algebra* which has been used earlier. Indeed, the requirement may easily be described by means of the truth table shown below.

p	t	*l*	*a*
low	low	low	low
low	low	high	low
low	high	low	high
low	high	high	high
high	low	low	low
high	low	high	low
high	high	low	low
high	high	high	high

The logical task that needs to be carried out may be expressed as:

a is high *if* (p is low *and* t is high *and* l is low),
or (p is low *and* t is high *and* l is high),
or (p is high *and* t is high *and* l is high).

In the shorthand of Boolean algebra this may be written as:

$$a = \bar{p}t\bar{l} + ptl + \bar{p}tl$$

where x reads x is high,
$\bar{x}$ reads x is not high (ie low),
xy reads x is high *and* y is high,
$x + y$ reads x is high *or* y is high.
(where x and y are binary variables like p, t and l)

It was Claude Shannon (1938) who pursued the idea that such logical operations could be performed by simple switches as shown in Figure 1.1.

In the contemporary world of the microchip such switches are made out of combinations of silicon and may occur in their millions on a single square centimetre of material.

However the point of this section is not to introduce microelectronics technology, but rather to explain what is meant when it is said (as will be in Chapters 2 and 3) that the appropriate mathematical medium for intelligent systems is logical, rather than the linear algebra conventionally used in engineering. In fact, it is likely that a system designer concerned with building 'intelligence' into engineering artefacts would not make direct use of the switching logic just described. It is more than likely, however, that he would know how to design logic switching circuits and thus have acquired a working knowledge of logical principles.

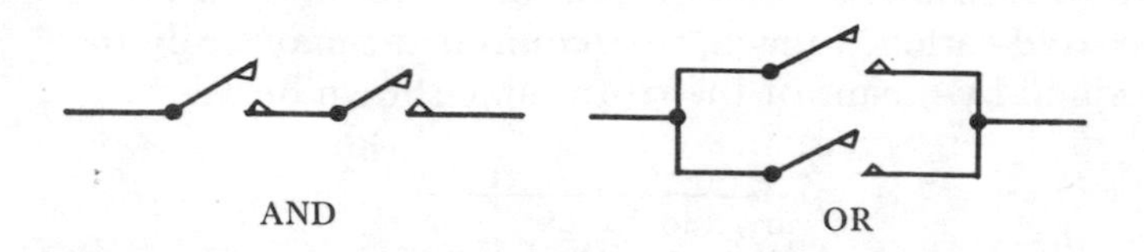

Figure 1.1. *The logic of switches: an AND gate is used in computer logic to combine binary signals in such a way that there is an output signal only if all input channels carry a signal, whereas an OR gate outputs a signal if any input channel carries a signal.*

The standpoint taken in this book is that the designer of intelligent systems will need a working knowledge of a particular development of the switching logic discussed above – that of automata theory.

COPING WITH MEMORY

Automata theory not only copes with the logical nature of intelligent processing, but also can represent 'memory'. Consider the following statement:

> Sound the alarm if the high pressure and low load suddenly reverse to low pressure and high load, but not if the latter state occurs after any other condition.

Clearly this kind of system needs to be not only logical but needs to have a memory of the previous state in order to operate properly. It is the presence of such memory that creates much of the fascination of intelligent systems. It creates that element of surprise, due to the internal, unseen, storage powers. It is for this reason that automata are discussed in Chapter 2 as 'systems with hidden complexity'.

A MATHEMATICAL UNDERSTANDING

The themes of memory and logic appear as central features throughout discussions on the design of intelligent systems. Consequently, it seems relevant to look more broadly at the nature of the mathematics of such notions.

Chapter 3 attempts to provide this background by taking a historical approach to this 'new' mathematics. Indeed, it was the break-away from Euclidean mathematics by pure mathematicians of the beginning of this century which saw significant transition from linear analysis into logic. Logic is implicit in *set theory* which dominated mathematical thinking during the beginning of the century. But what of memory?

This enters the mathematical picture through the question: 'How does the *amount* of memory affect the behaviour of a logic/memory system?' The answer is that memory is that which mediates between the stimulus and the response of an intelligent system. The effect of this is to group together sequences of stimuli which lead the system into the same internal memory state. This type of investigation finds a parallel in the new mathematics as 'semi-group systems'. A semi-group is one of the many algebraic systems studied during the last 50 years by pure mathematicians. Such systems are broadly described in Chapter 3, so as to dispel the feeling that the theoretical background to intelligent systems is isolated or in any way spurious.

COPING WITH LANGUAGE

Probably the most distinctive addition to the body of mathematics made by automata theoreticians (rather than the other way round) is the extension of this type of mathematics to include the representation of the structure of language. Best known is the contribution of Chomsky (1957) who extended and specialized general notions of automata theory to the creation of a mathematical structure related to the rules of a language. It is undeniable that an intelligent system will have to be sensitive to a language of some kind. This could be a highly contrived language, such as is used to program computers, or something closer to natural language. Chapter 3 concludes with the mathematical background to this.

COPING WITH REALITY

No apology is made for the step taken in Chapter 5, where the practical problems of a potential field of application for intelligent systems are discussed. This may seem an abrupt step from considerations of the mathematical background and the computational problems for intelligent systems, but in a sense it does bring some seemingly disparate topics together. In particular, several stages in the development of vision for robots are singled out so as to show how vision automata and artificial intelligence systems need to be combined so as to create a system that is at least intelligent enough to understand the requirements of a production engineer or an operator, without them needing to become program designers.

COPING WITH THE FUTURE

Chapter 7 can be seen as an opportunity to take a specific glimpse into the future of intelligent systems design. It is argued that it may be possible to achieve a necessary degree of intentionality in an engineered system if an experience-gathering machine could be designed. Later a particular theory of experience-gathering in humans is scrutinized and related to design principles discussed in earlier parts of the book. This is presented as merely one of the avenues open to the designer of intelligent systems of the future.

CHAPTER 2

Systems with hidden complexity

There is an important factor that distinguishes objects such as a cup, a billiard ball, a pencil and a book, from objects such as a human being, a cat, a clockwork mouse and a computer. The latter all have *inner mechanisms* that determine their behaviour, while the former will have a behaviour that has no hidden aspects. A billiard ball will roll predictably down an inclined plane, but even as simple a device as a clockwork mouse holds some surprises as one cannot predict its behaviour immediately from looking at it, not without knowing whether the spring is in a wound or unwound state.

Systems designers call such devices *automata;* the dictionary refers to these as 'devices endowed with inner motion'. Clearly, before the evolution of systems that have information rather than energy as their life-blood, machines were seen as having either overt or inner *motion.* The word motion can, in the case of informational machines, be replaced by terms such as 'computational power' or 'logical operations'. Indeed, it will be seen that the most general mechanism for this inner activity is memory. A simple example might help at this stage.

Think of approaching a cat with a bowl of food, or with an empty bowl. Were the cat merely to respond automatically, it would eat when the bowl was full and not eat when the bowl was empty. In fact, it may be difficult to predict whether the cat will eat or not because its internal state may be anywhere between starving and satiated. A system designer could develop a simple automaton model to explain the way in which the internal state relates to the input and the output.

Part of the simplification centres on a precise definition of the following quantities:

input: this is the set (empty bowl, full bowl),
output: this is the set (eats, does not eat),
states: this is the set (satiated, neutral, starving).

The last of the three definitions could obviously have contained more states: it is the designer's choice to use only a simple representation, sufficient to the needs of his explanation.

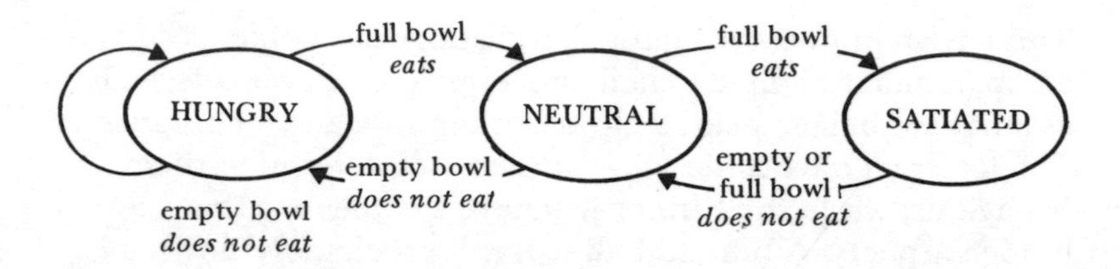

Figure 2.1. *A state transition diagram can be used to determine all possible actions of the cat with regard to its feeding habits*

Figure 2.1 illustrates a *state transition diagram* for this situation. Clearly, the circles represent the internal states, while the arrows show how the states change depending on particular inputs and outputs. Thus, the transition between the neutral and the satiated state may be interpreted as: 'in the neutral state, if the cat finds a full bowl and eats, it will become satiated.' This enables us to express very clearly the notion that the cat will only refuse food when in the satiated state. The only part of the behaviour of the system that is not clear in such a diagram is the timing of the events. There is an implicit assumption in state diagrams that states can change only at specific times. For example, in the present case, one hour intervals may be appropriate.

The central importance of the description of systems with inner complexity by means of automata lies in the descriptive powers that are offered by such schemes. For example, American psychologist B.F. Skinner is seen as the founder of a school of thought called *behaviourism.* The essence of the descriptive techniques used within that school relies on trying to describe complex living systems, including human beings, in terms of stimulus-response patterns. This is supported by experiments on animals in which they are taught to 'peck at the right door' when presented with a meaningless symbol, such as a green triangle. This sort of philosophy denies the vast amount of internal information processing that may go on in a living being. The automata theoretician, on the other hand, stands back in awe at this complexity and offers a way of describing it. Obviously no one would claim to be able to map the complete state diagram of the inner complexity of a cat, let alone a human being. It is the fact that it is possible to talk of this inner complexity on a secure descriptive footing that is important.

There is another very important facet of automata-like descriptions of systems: they provide a basis for designing things at the level of description such as shown in Figure 2.1. That is, the description does not involve the flesh and bones of the cat, only the pertinent parts of its behaviour. If one is designing informational systems, the automata-based description provides a way of getting the design right before one even starts worrying about its physical representation. State structures of the type shown in Figure 2.1 may be implemented in a variety of ways, including the use of programs in a computer or the engineering of circuits.

In the rest of this chapter we shall first take a closer look at the essentials of state diagrams that relate to machine design, then look at an example of the way a design may be understood by a progressive build-up of its state diagram. Finally, we shall return to the use of automata to model situations that are less machine-like.

The formal automaton

There are four distinct aspects of the design of a machine that concern the designer: the machine specification, the state diagram, a tabular statement of the state diagram and finally some means of implementation. Consider the state diagram in Figure 2.2 as a starting point of an illustration.

Instead of going from specification to design as an automata designer would have to do, we shall attempt the process in reverse: going from the diagram in Figure 2.2 to a verbal statement of what the machine is doing. First, it is possible to identify the three key sets of the automaton:

the input set: 1, 2, 3,
the output set: x, y,
and the state set: A, B, C, D.

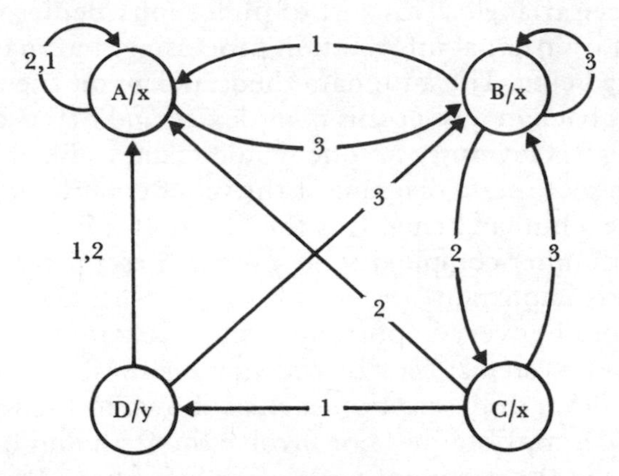

Figure 2.2. *A state diagram for a machine, where 1 – 3 is the input set, x and y the output set and A – D the state set*

Before reading on, the reader might care to study Figure 2.1 for a while and try to describe the function of the machine. If this proves to be too difficult, the best way to proceed is to imagine a stream of input, and note the resulting output:

input: 132113321312332122221132132321313221322111
output: xxxyxxxxyxxxxxxyxxxxxxxxyxxxxyxxxxxxxxxyxx

It now becomes quite easy to note that the system is a detector of the sequence 321. It normally outputs x, except in cases where 321 has occurred where it outputs y when the 1 is input. In fact, this last sentence may be taken as the specification of the system.

In heading for some sort of implementation of this machine, it becomes convenient to specify the relationship between the elements of the three sets in tabular form, as shown in Figure 2.3.

Several things should be noted about this representation. First, both in Figure 2.2 and 2.3, the output is associated with the state. This was not the case with Figure 2.1, where the outputs were associated with the arrows on the diagram. Both of these methods are used, Figure 2.1 being typical of a Mealy model, and Figure 2.2 of a Moore model, after the original proposers of these systems. The message here is not to worry about such differences, the resulting models may be shown to be equivalent to one another.

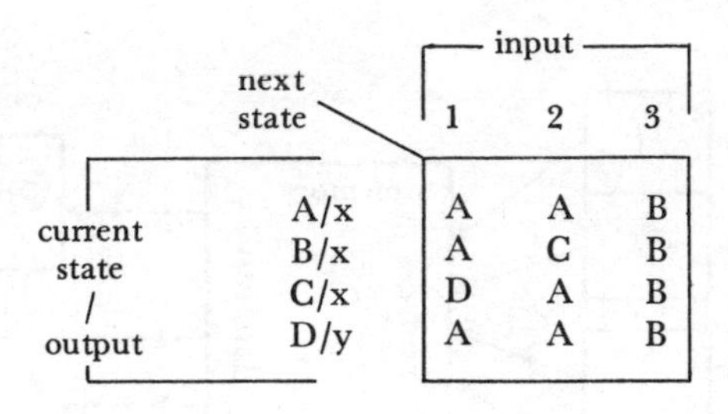

Figure 2.3. *A state table for the machine illustrated in Figure 2.2*

The second, and more obvious observation is that, given *i* inputs in the input set, and *s* states in the state set, it is necessary to specify (i x s) next states in the table in order to say exactly what the system is doing.

Given a state table one can think of a great variety of methods for actually building a machine to behave in the way that the automaton model indicates. These could range from the use of construction kits to the use of a computer program. Here we shall be concerned with only two possible methods: electronic implementation and a computer program. It is worth stressing, however, that the power of automata models derives from the fact that much of the hard thought about design goes into structuring the automaton (this will be discussed in detail later) while implementation into a working device is an almost automatic procedure.*

Electronically, all that is needed is a memory chip (this could be of the read-only type if the machine is being made once-and-for-all, otherwise a read-write memory could be used). Memories have two essential parts, the address part and the data-out part (the data-in part is not important here). The address is like the label on a filing cabinet pocket, while

* Readers who are not too familiar with electronics or programming should skip to the next section.

the data-out part is like the contents of the pocket. All these data exist in binary code. In addition, three registers (temporary stores) are needed to store the input address, the output data and the state data. The complete arrangement is shown in Figure 2.4.

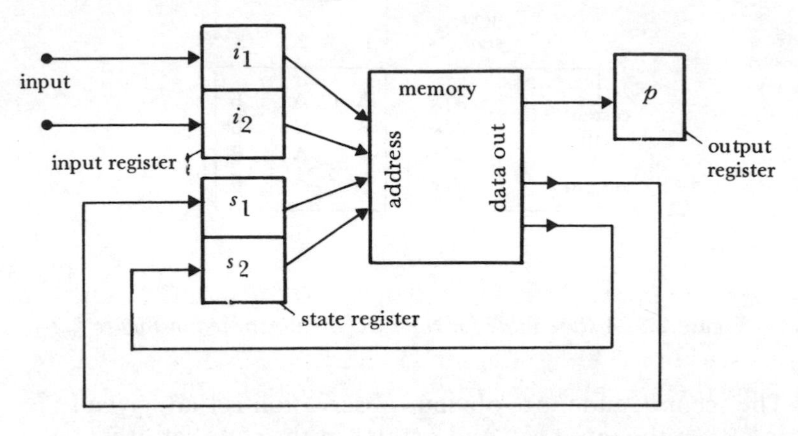

Figure 2.4. *A hardware implementation: the three registers are used to store the input address, the state data and the output data*

The essence of the electronic design is that the symbols of the automaton are coded into binary values. These then reside in the registers as data that either addresses the memory or is received from it (as in the case of the output). The state register both addresses the memory and receives data. Clearly, this arrangement requires a careful distribution of timing information. This is beyond the need of the current explanation which concentrates on the logical function of the system.* It can be seen that two connections have been allowed for the coding of the input messages, say:

input	*coding*	
	i_1	i_2
1	0	1
2	1	0
3	1	1

It can be seen that the input code (0 0) is not used. Similarly,

* Any one of the many textbooks available on the design of logic circuits will provide such background.

the state messages may be coded as:

state	*coding*	
	s_1	s_2
A	0	0
B	0	1
C	1	0
D	1	1

In this case, all the possible binary codes are used. The output may simply be coded as:

output	*coding*
	p
x	0
y	1

There are no hard-and-fast rules about the choice of these coding schemes and, as can be seen, they have been arbitrarily chosen. In the literature on switching system design there are some theories regarding the optimization of coding for the states. The aim of such theories is to discover codes that allow one to use several smaller memories in place of the one large one. Such schemes go under the title of *the state assignment problem.* Again, this is beyond the scope of this text.

In order to make the system work, it becomes a simple matter of inserting the right binary information into the memory. Physically, this process depends on the kind of memory that is being used. Read-only memories have ways of 'burning-in' this information once-and-for-all, while read-write memories (or 'volatile' memories as they are sometimes called) need to have the information read in every time that the system is switched on. In principle, however, returning to the filing cabinet model, the information contained in Figure 2.3 can be used to derive the addresses (pocket labels) and contents of the memory, through the intermediary of the codes described earlier. Because there are three output wires from the memory, the contents of each location (pocket) are expressed as three binary digits. The addresses are expressed as four binary digits, and the complete content is shown in Figure 2.5.

The meaning of this table is, taking the seventh line as an example, when the input is 1 (coded as i_1,i_2=0,1) and the state C (coded as s_1, s_2=1,0) the next state code is 1,1, namely state D, with its corresponding output 1, that is, y. This corresponds to the first entry in the third row of the table in Figure 2.3 and the output associated with D. The memory entries labelled d (for 'don't care') are irrelevant, since the input i_1,i_2=0,0 will never be used.

addresses				*data out*		
i_1	i_2	s_1	s_2	s_1	s_2	p
0	0	0	0	d	d	d
0	0	0	1	d	d	d
0	0	1	0	d	d	d
0	0	1	1	d	d	d
0	1	0	0	0	0	0
0	1	0	1	0	0	0
0	1	1	0	1	1	1
0	1	1	1	0	0	0
1	0	0	0	0	0	0
1	0	0	1	1	0	0
1	0	1	0	0	0	0
1	0	1	1	0	0	0
1	1	0	0	0	1	0
1	1	0	1	0	1	0
1	1	1	0	0	1	0
1	1	1	1	0	1	0

Figure 2.5. *Memory content for the circuit shown in Figure 2.4*

Now for a software implementation – surprisingly this is easier to follow than the hardware implementation, given an elementary knowledge of some computer language. No particular computer language will be used here, but instruction styles that are common to all languages will be referred to. In fact, there is only one type of instruction that is needed to do the whole job. This is: 'If (logical event j) then (logical event k).' These logical events are statements joined by the prepositions AND and OR and include the use of NOT. In the implementation of automata these statements take an even more standardized form: 'If (state X and input Y) then (next state W and output Z).'

Each such statement corresponds to an entry in a table such as that shown in Figure 2.3. Using this figure, and working from left to right and downwards, gives 12 statements – as shown opposite.

Clearly, if there is a means for reading the sequence of inputs and recording the sequence of outputs, this software automaton would behave according to the specification.

If (state	A and input	1) then (next state	A and output	x)	1
	A	2	A	x	2
	A	3	B	x	3
	⋮				⋮
	C	1	D	y	7
	⋮				⋮
	D	2	A	x	11
	D	3	B	x	12

A DESIGN EXAMPLE

Having argued that given an automaton state diagram or state table, the transfer into working machinery is a fairly mechanical procedure, this section concentrates on the creation of such diagrams from a given specification. This is not a mechanical procedure by any means. It embodies many of the features of creativity that are required for any form of design. The difficulty lies in the fact that a specification may be simply stated at the level of a desired input-output behaviour of an automaton, providing virtually no clues as to the state relationships that are required.

For instance, the following specification is to be met:

A combination lock for a safe is to be designed. The input symbols are (A,B,S,F) and the outputs are (no,op,al). The latter stand for do *no*thing, *op*en the safe and sound an *al*arm, respectively. It is understood by all concerned (safe owners and burglars, that is) that any attempt at opening the safe will start with the input symbol S (start) and end with the input symbol F (finish). The string of symbols in between will consist of As and Bs only. Now, only the safe owner knows that in order to open the safe, he must apply an *even palendromic* string of As and Bs.

An even palendromic string is one with an even number of symbols where the second half of the string is a reversed version of the first half. Strings such as ABBA, AAAA, ABAAAABBAAAABA are even palendromic while ABBBBAA, BAAABA, ABA are not. The last of these is, in fact, *odd palendromic.* Of course, to open the safe, a string would have to be applied as SABBAF, where S and F are signals to the system meaning start and finish.

It is interesting that at this point, a very simple solution to this problem suggests itself in practical terms. Those who know a little about programming would easily be able to implement the solution on a computer. It is this: record the string and count the number of symbols between S and F. If this is odd sound the alarm, if it is even pair off the symbols working from the outer symbols inward, and sound the alarm if the pairing does not work out. The safe can only be opened if the pairing works out for the whole string. For example, the string SABAAF would first pass on the length count, then pass on the pairing of the first and last symbol, but fail when the next two symbols B and A are compared.

To be awkward, and to serve the interest of illustrating design at the state-diagram level, we can object to the above solution in two ways. First, it is too specific. Although it is a very specific programming solution, it does not fit with the general hardware and software models discussed in the previous section. Second, the assessment of the string should really be done 'on-the-fly', ie as the string is being presented. Then the system could be expected to react as the last F is input rather than having to wait for further computation.

Returning to the level of design of the state diagram of the required system (or *state structure* as opposed to physical structure) it becomes clear that the ill-defined length of the string is going to be a problem. That is, if the automaton is being activated on-the-fly, it will have no information at any point during its action as to how much more of the string is going to be input. Therefore, it is not possible to gain a clear idea of how many states need to be used.

It is common practice in design, when the specification seems to be too difficult to tackle all at once, to set an intermediary target which is more easily achieved. Even though this will not produce the required result, the designer expects to learn more about the problem, so as to enable him to push his target on towards the final goal. In the present case, quite a drastic simplification is made to the specification. Initially, it was assumed that the length of the string between S and F is precisely four symbols.

The leftmost state of this automaton (see Figure 2.6) is entered whenever the symbol S is input. It can be seen that states D, E, F and G represent all possible length-two sequences of 1s and 0s. From these positions it is only the reversed strings that lead to state J, which in turn, upon an input of F, leads to state M, the only one labelled *op,* so allowing the safe to be opened. State K, on the other hand, collects entries from all those inputs beyond the centre of the diagram that deviate from the palindrome (the transitions from H and I, 2 and 1, respectively, also go to K, but have been omitted so as not to clutter the diagram).

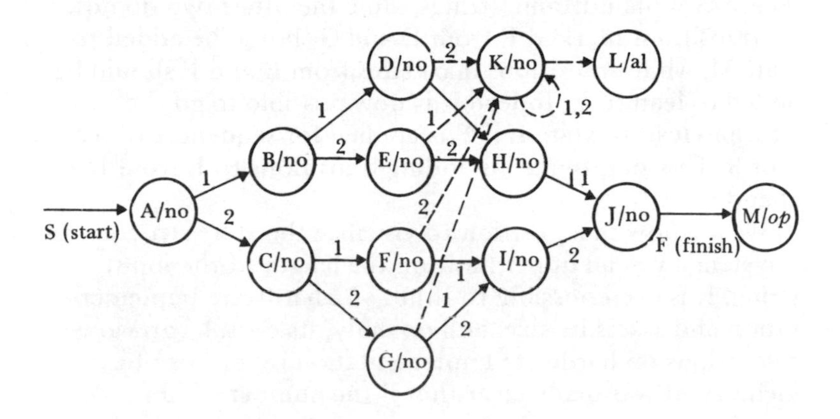

Figure 2.6. *State diagram for a four-symbol automaton: note the symmetric pattern of the state structure*

The most notable feature of what has been done so far, is the symmetric pattern of the state structure for this task. This gives a considerable insight into the structure of the automaton for any fixed string length. Indeed, it is possible to develop a knowledge of the number of states that are required for even palindromes of length x (x being any even integer). First, it should be noted that states K, M and L will be there, over and above the symmetrical part of the rest of the structure. The symmetrical part grows in a regular although somewhat hard-to-enumerate fashion. To understand this growth, consider the number of states in the centre column — this can be seen to be $2^{x/2}$. It is not so easy to see that the group to the left of the centre column grows with x as $2^{x/2}-1$. The total number of states (Q) is $3 + 2^{x/2} + 2(2^{x/2}-1)$ which may be written as $1 + 3 \times 2^{x/2}$.

At this point it is quite easy to extend the design to cover strings shorter than x. Since it is the value of x that determines the shape of the state structure, shorter strings may be assessed not by changing the state structure in any way, but by adding new transitions within the existing structure. For example, in Figure 2.6, the only string length shorter than four that needs to be considered is two. Therefore, if the F input were applied after two inputs, one would be at the level of states D, E, F and G. Of those four, D and G represent length-two palindromic strings while the other two do not. So transitions marked F from D and G should be added to state M, while transitions marked F from E and F should be added to lead to L. Indeed it is now possible to go the whole way and lead to state L if F is applied for sequences of length 1 or 3. This simply means adding transitions to L from B, C, H and I.

We are now in a position to visualize the state structure of a system given an upper limit on the length of the input string. It is even possible to think of a hardware implementation and assess its size, and possibly, its cost. In previous discussions on hardware implementation by means of a memory, it was made clear that if the number of items handled by the memory (ie states, inputs or outputs) is *n*, then the size of the relevant register is $/\log_2 n/$ and $/c/$ is the notation for 'the least integer greater than *c*'. In this case it is easy to see that the size of the input register is 1, and the output register is 2, and the number of input and output items is 2 and 3, respectively.

Using the previously derived formula for the number of states (Q):

$$Q = 1 + 3x2^{x/2}$$

it can be shown that the size of the state register needs to be at most:

$$\frac{x}{2} + 2$$

Now, referring back to Figure 2.4, the number of address terminals of the memory needs to be:

$$\frac{x}{2} + 3$$

to account for the input register as well.

The cost of a system may be said to be roughly proportional to the number of bits in the memory. In general, for a memory with A address terminals and D data-out terminals the amount of memory is $2^A \times D$ bits. In the present case, it has been seen that A is X/2 + 3, and D is X/2 + 5 (to account for the two output terminals). So, choosing some arbitrary value of x, say 12, it is possible to calculate the required amount of storage, which turns out to be 5632 bits. Even though the cost of a bit changes from day to day, it can be seen that the method of state structure design has enabled us to come a long way towards the engineering solution.

However, the problem has not been solved completely, and for any length of string. If 'any length' means a string of infinite length, then this cannot be done with a finite number of states since the cost formula would evaluate to infinity. This is also true of the simple engineering solution given earlier. In fact, the hidden barb in the specification has been a demand for infinite cost. However, the design sequence followed here would have enabled the designer to feed back to the specifier, this flaw in the specification.

To recap, two fundamental lessons have been demonstrated by this design exercise; first, that the abstract mode of expression in terms of state diagrams enables the limitations of the machine to be determined. These are *theoretical* limitations that are likely to constrain any implementation. Second, this increased understanding allows the designer to refine and correct the specification.

The modelling power of automata

So far the state structure has been shown to be a useful medium in which the creative process of design can take place. Now two examples will be considered in which the state structure is used as a modelling tool. The object here is to clarify and predict the behaviour of systems whose inner complexity is such as to mask a clear view of the system's function. The first example is one in which the strategies of three parties interact. Although this will be presented as a simple card game, it is the kind of situation that might occur in business, engineering systems or even the strategy of warfare. The second example will deal with a notoriously difficult area for modelling: the psychology of dreams.

THE CARD GAME

Seated around a table are three players and a referee. The players can use cards of two colours: red (r) and green (g). At any point in time the players each have a card, with its colour showing, on the table in front of them. Each player decides what colour card he will next place on the table, on the basis of a rule which he alone uses, each player using his own personal rule. When the referee blows a whistle each player changes the card in front of him according to the decision he has already made. If this were to be played as a game, the players would, in turn, have an opportunity to deal out a complete set of three cards of their own choice. At any point in the game, a player may elect to shout 'play' instead of taking his turn at dealing the cards. At this point, he must write down on a piece of paper his prediction for the eventual outcome of the game which is played without further individual dealings of cards. If the player is right he gains a point, if he is wrong he loses one. Another round may then start in which the players decide new rules for themselves.

It is not the intention here to get involved in the strategy for playing the game, but merely to find an appropriate automaton model that will provide an insight into what goes on during such a game. First, it is clear that the state of the system is the set of three cards on the table. There are, therefore, eight possible states that could occur. To go on, three typical rules can be defined that the players may have chosen for themselves:

Player 1 (P1): plays a (r)ed card if and only if players 1 *and* 2 are (r)ed in the previous state,
Player 2 (P2): plays the card opposite to that played by player 1 in the previous state,
Player 3 (P3): plays (r)ed if and only if players 2 *and* 3 are (g)reen in the previous state.

A complete state table may now be drawn embodying these rules. It should be noted that the next state only depends on the previous state, ie this is an automaton with no input. Also there is no specific output, although the state itself may be considered as such – see Figure 2.7.

Perhaps more interesting is the state structure that can be derived from this table – see Figure 2.8.

One noticeable feature of this state diagram is that each state has just one exit which, because of a lack of input,

current state			*next state*		
P2	P1	P2	P1	P2	P3
g	g	g	g	r	r
g	g	r	g	r	g
g	r	g	g	r	g
g	r	r	g	r	g
r	g	g	g	g	r
r	g	r	g	g	g
r	r	g	r	g	g
r	r	r	r	g	g

Figure 2.7. *State table for the card game, g = green card and r = red card*

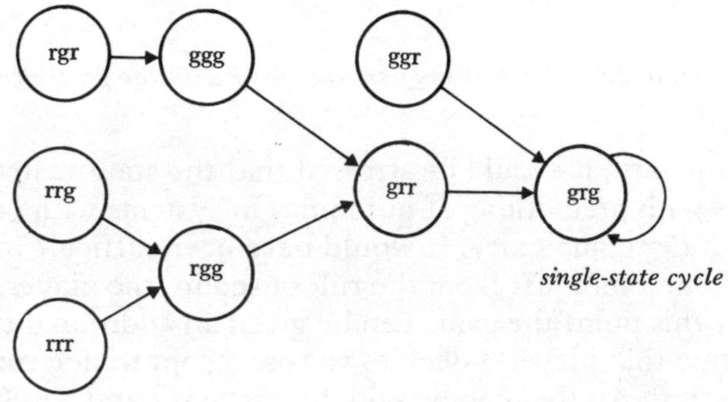

Figure 2.8. *State diagram for the card game derived from Figure 2.7*

remains unlabelled. Such inputless automata are called *autonomous.* Figure 2.7 shows that whenever the game gets into the *play* phase, it will always end in state grg and remain there. State grg is called a *single-state cycle.* In fact it is a characteristic of all autonomous automata that in the long run, they enter a cycle of states involving more than one state. This can be illustrated by changing the rule for P2 slightly:

Player 2: plays the card opposite to that played by player 1 in the previous state, except when the state is grr.

Clearly, this affects only one transition, grr; instead of going to grg it now goes to ggg. This results in the state diagram shown in Figure 2.9.

It should be noted that the behaviour of the system divides neatly into two modes. If play starts in any of the states, rgr ggg grr rgg rrg rrr, then the cycle consisting of repetitions of ggg and grr will be the final outcome. On the other hand, if the state at the play point is either grg or ggr, the outcome is the single-state grg cycle.

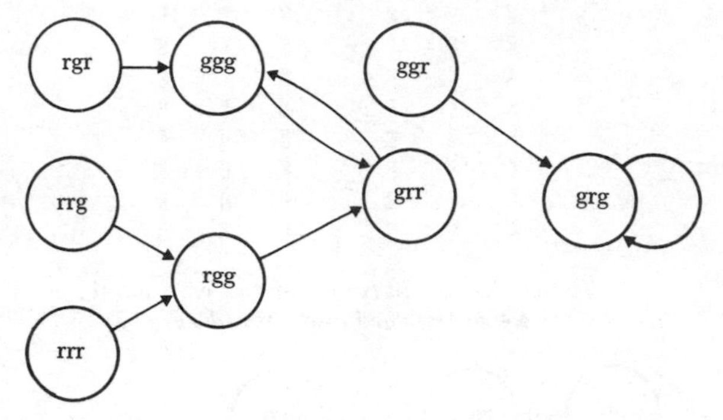

Figure 2.9. *Effect of the new rule for P2 on the grr transition*

In summary, it should be stressed that the state structure helps with predictions of outcomes in systems with considerable inner complexity. It would have been difficult to predict such outcomes just from the rules used by the players.

At this point the game can be given an additional twist. Assume that player 3 decides to toss a coin to determine his next card. All that can be said now is that r and g in the third position occur with a probability of 0.5 each. An automaton model used to resolve statistical situations of this kind, is called *probabilistic.* It differs in the sense that now the probability of making a transition is shown on the transition arrows. For example, state ggg can now lead to states grr and grg with an equal probability of 0.5. This may easily be illustrated in the state structure – see Figure 2.10.

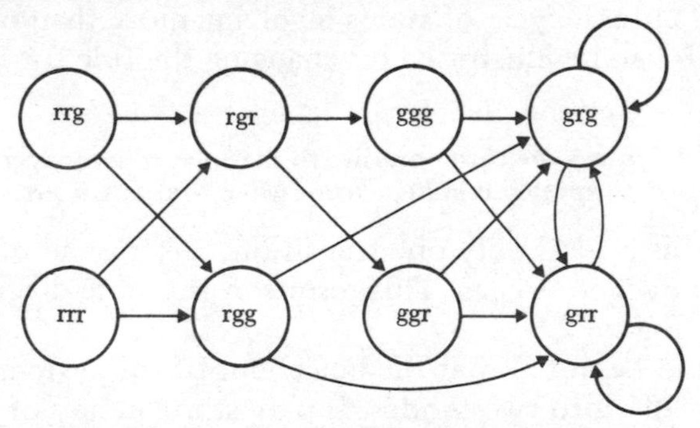

Figure 2.10. *The probabilistic automaton used to resolve statistical situations in the card game*

It should be noted that while player 3 is following his probabilistic strategy, players 1 and 2 are following the original rules, as for the state structure illustrated in Figure 2.8.

One might think that the random behaviour of player 3 might prevent any lucid description of the system's behaviour. A glance at Figure 2.10 will show that this is not so. First notice that there is a general drift in the diagram from left to right. It is possible to make even more positive statements. Say that it is known that play commences in state rrr. After one round, the probabilities of the system being in either state rgr or rgg are 0.5 and 0.5. The next round is slightly more complicated. There are four possible outcomes: ggg grg ggr and grr. The division of probabilities is ggr 0.25, grg 0.25, ggg 0.25 and grr 0.25.

In this way one can assign probabilities to restricted sets of states at any round of the game. Indeed, it is not difficult to see that after four steps, the probability of being in any one but the two rightmost states is zero, while the probability of actually being in either state grg or grr is 0.5.

To conclude this section on card playing it should be stressed that modelling by means of state structures can provide considerable insight into situations where there is an interaction between elements that follow separate strategies. This is of relevance to intelligent systems, as it points to human activities such as stock markets, economies and even international diplomacy.

A DREAMING AUTOMATON

Undeniably, the process of dreaming in humans is one of the most fascinating by-products of inner complexity. It is not the object of this section to develop a complete psychological theory of the phenomenon, but merely to use it as an illustration of the flexibility of automata models.

It is quite possible to relate the colloquial term 'mental state' to the formal states of the machines described so far. The mental state of a human being has precisely the attributes of its machine counterpart. Imagine a mental state 'thinking about what to have for breakfast'. This might have been as a result of an autonomous transition from being in a 'just woken up' state, or be driven from an environmental input.

In Figure 2.11 a sketch has been made of some of the mental states that may be encountered during the first and last parts of a day, and some of the environmental inputs that may be responsible for entering these states.

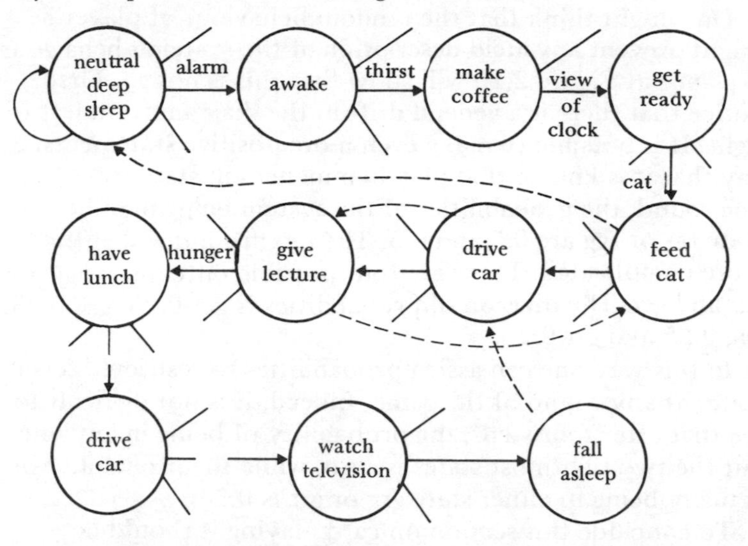

Figure 2.11. *A trajectory through mental states; the solid lines represent controlled state changes and the dashed lines those transitions that are not controlled – such as when dreaming*

This is a highly simplified sketch, and anything but complete. The solid transitions show where controlled state changes take place. In some cases, the input event is shown in the diagram, in others the changes may be autonomous or just not specified. Naturally, if a living creature were to be represented fully in this way, one would need a very large number of states. A functional system achieves its function by being able to change states in a limited number of ways, ie from any one state, only a number of states that is much smaller than the total may be reached. Which one is actually used depends on an input (or lack thereof). This means that there are *distances* associated with the state structure itself. It is possible to define such a distance between two states as the shortest number of transitions that may be found in going from one state to the other.

In Figure 2.11 it is assumed that there is a mental state 'neutral deep sleep'. This corresponds to a state of 'relaxation' of the system which, by referring back to Figure 2.4, can be given a technical meaning. In this state, there is no doubt that the brain is insensitive to environmental inputs. This is a physical process such as closing one's eyes. One cannot close one's ears, but it is for this reason that most living creatures seek quiet places in which to sleep. What this means in Figure 2.4 is that such a state could be simulated by ensuring that inputs such as i_1 and i_2 remain unchanging.

But sleep is not only about being cut off from environmental input. In the same way as the inputs become unchanging due to a physical relaxation process, the state input (s_1 and s_2) also go to an unchanging, 'neutral' state. This then is the first state in Figure 2.11.

After being woken up by an alarm clock, say, the process of state transitions can be seen as a state 'trajectory' that is getting further and further away from the neutral state. Upon falling asleep therefore, the process of relaxation may be seen as a return to the neutral state from a distant part of the state structure. The transitions are no longer controlled, and could take a meandering path such as shown by the dashed line in Figure 2.11. In this case, the state transitions may manifest themselves as a dream which might feel like 'driving a car through a lecture room full of cats'. The return trajectory could also get into states that have not been experienced during waking hours for some years.

This model has several properties that are known to be true of dreams. For example, it may be possible to recall a dream only if the dreamer is awakened during a return trajectory, as upon returning to the neutral state, the trajectory may have been forgotten due to its weak links. It is known that people dream several times during a period of sleep, in regular on-off cycles. In the model described here this would be explained as a physiological cycle of greater or lesser relaxation of the state inputs. During periods of lesser relaxation the automaton would begin to take autonomous trips through its state structure, not as controlled as during waking hours, but entering 'learnt' states, so as to give an illusion of reality.

It is feasible that even a machine might have a *need* to dream, because, were the neutral state not reached during sleep, it might be much more difficult to enter a sympathetic set of states if prematurely awakened, than if complete relaxation had taken place. This might explain why subjects who are deprived of dreams (in contrast to being deprived of sleep) display considerable confusion in coping with the real world.

Summary

The crux of this chapter has been the way in which it is possible to model systems that have a hidden, inner complexity. However, the object of this book is not solely a description of the modelling of systems that may somehow be described as being intelligent, but also a discussion of the design of such systems. The modelling powers of automata have been illustrated and it has been shown that such abstract devices may be translated either into hardware or software by standard procedures.

However, there are a few doubts over this simple model. For instance, it may be possible to approach the design of intelligent systems much more directly, say, by defining an intelligent task and then writing a program to execute it. This point will be discussed fully in Chapter 4. Further, the question then arises of whether automata have any fundamental role to play in the design of intelligent systems. The exact nature of this will be explored in Chapter 3 from a standpoint of enquiring how and why the sort of abstraction found in automata is *ever* useful. This raises the question of the role of mathematical modelling, as opposed to software design.

CHAPTER 3

Mathematical modelling

Engineers and scientists are known to be heavy 'users' of mathematics. The point under discussion here is whether a designer of intelligent systems is likely to use mathematics, and if so, what branch of mathematics this would be. The answer is positive, in the sense that much of the thought that goes into a design may be abstract and symbolic. The branch of mathematics closest to this is termed abstract or modern algebra. Realizing that this is a branch of mathematics that is usually called *pure,* its possible application comes as a surprise to the pure mathematician, engineer and scientist alike. The latter has a store of knowledge in mathematics that would normally be called *applied,* whilst the engineer may find it disturbing that the 'purity' may become tainted by application.

The 'modernity' of abstract algebras comes from the mathematical revolution that took place at the beginning of this century, with the realization that Euclidian geometry, and its re-framing as algebra (of the classical kind), was only one mathematical system among a possible infinity of other systems. The nature of these other systems is that their validity is judged on the excellence of the logic that links the points of departure (axioms) to important properties (theorems). In classical mathematics validity is normally sought in the predictions that are made about effects that can be measured in the real world. In broad terms it is the freedom with which axioms may be selected that is appealing to the intelligent systems designer, and it is for this reason that his method of mathematical expression may be closer to the modern rather than the classical. In what follows a distinction will be created between these two modes and examples will be given of the ways that modern algebra can be used.

The use of classical mathematics

The ways in which classical mathematics can be used will be considered first. Take the case of a simple pendulum: a mass (m) suspended from a long inflexible string (of length L) and displaced from its central hanging position by a small amount (x).

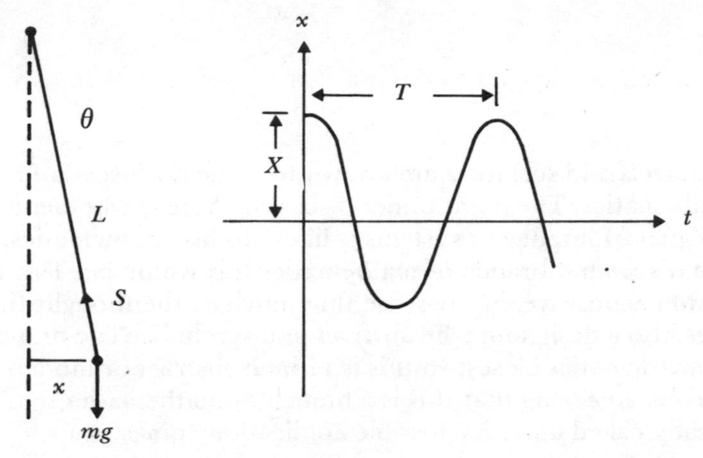

Figure 3.1. *A prediction of pendulum action x with time t: simple harmonic oscillation at period T*

The prediction of what happens to the mass involves a mixture of physical laws, algebra and calculus. First, according to Newton's laws of conservation of energy, the horizontal and vertical forces in the system must balance:

for vertical forces: $S \cos\theta = mg$
for horizontal forces: $S \sin\theta = -mf$

Here Newton's law of motion (that force = mass x acceleration) is used, g being the acceleration due to gravity, and f the acceleration in the horizontal direction of the mass itself. S is the tension in the string while $S \cos\theta$ and $S \sin\theta$ are the parts of that tension acting vertically and norizontally, respectively. Trigonometry is used in the formulation of these last two expressions. By approximation and simplification, based on the fact that θ can be very acute, the following equation can be formulated:

$$-\frac{d^2x}{dt^2} = \frac{gx}{L}$$

where x is the distance of the mass from the vertical. This deceptively simple expression is a differential equation. Differential calculus, which deals with rates of change, was invented by Isaac Newton in the seventeenth century and virtually revolutionized mathematics. A solution to this equation yields the desired variation of x with time:

$$x = X \cos wt$$

where w is an angular frequency equal to $2\pi/T$. Also:

$$T = 2\pi(L/g)^{1/2}$$

In some ways the last equation may be a little unexpected. It predicts that the time for one oscillation is independent of the mass of the pendulum. Indeed, if one were to carry out an experiment with different masses, the truth of this result could be borne out. Other truths of this kind could also be tested by experiment. The crux of the matter is that for two thousand years it has been thought that this sort of real-world prediction of behaviour of physical entities was the evidence necessary to confirm the validity of the mathematics.

The demise of classical mathematics as a foundation

The happy relationship between abstraction and real-world effects came under threat during the first half of the nineteenth century, when mathematicians such as Lobatchevsky and Bolyai began questioning the generality of Euclid's starting point in geometry. Most of us have probably had some experience of Euclidean geometry at school. One of the fundamental starting points of this that has always seemed eminently reasonable is the axiom:

> 'Given a straight line AB and a point P not on this straight line, there is one and only one other straight line through P that is parallel to AB.'

Figure 3.2 illustrates the way in which this axiom could be questioned.

Imagine a line QR which goes through P as shown. Now imagine that this line pivots about P in the direction of the arrow, in a smooth and continuous fashion. There must come a point when this line becomes parallel to AB. At this point, if one were to believe in the axiom of parallel lines quoted earlier, either PQ ceases to exist, or the original parallel line

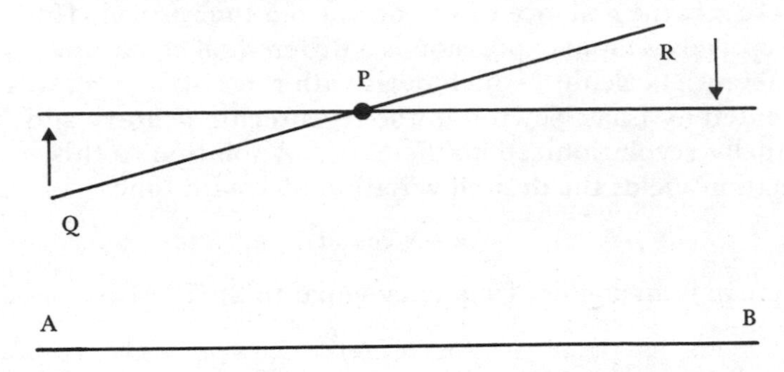

Figure 3.2. *How many lines through P are parallel to AB?*

disappears. Neither of these events is catered for by Euclidean geometry, which has no provision for lines appearing and disappearing. Putting aside the fact that Bolyai developed a new system of geometry in which there could be more than one line parallel to another passing through a common point, this argument sowed the seed in the minds of mathematicians that relying on common experience of the physical world may not be a good way to assess the truth of mathematical abstraction. This realization had a shattering effect on the world of mathematics. After all, the sheer survival power of mathematical notions put this science at a par with religion, and to question the foundations of such thoughts was seen as being profane.

Set theory

This realization gave rise to notions that now go under the heading of modern or abstract algebra, where Euclidean ideas are seen as being one mathematical system among many other such possible systems. This left one difficulty. Since the notion of *real numbers* seemed so fundamental and deeply engrained in classical mathematics, was its importance being questioned? George Cantor is usually credited as having resolved this problem at the turn of the twentieth century. He replaced the concept of number by the concept of a *set* as being the foundation stone for general mathematical systems.

A set is defined as a collection of objects. Whether an object belongs to a particular set is defined either by a property that it has in common with the other members of the set, or by being named as a member of that set. An example of the former definition of a set is 'the set of all cows'. The second definition produces sets such as 'the set consisting of Fred, Jack and Mary'.

The operations in set theory are very simple and are shown below:

1) the conjunction (read as OR, and uses the symbol $\cup$) which produces a set that contains all the elements of the two sets that have been conjoined;
2) the disjunction (read as AND, and uses the symbol $\cap$) which produces a set that contains all the elements that are common to the two sets that have been disjoined;
3) the negation (read as NOT, and uses the symbol –) which produces a set that excludes all the elements of the set that have been negated.

It is often the case that the validity of certain results of set theory are confirmed by means of diagrams. For example, in Figure 3.3, the following equality is confirmed:

$$(A \cap B) \cup (A \cap - B) = A$$

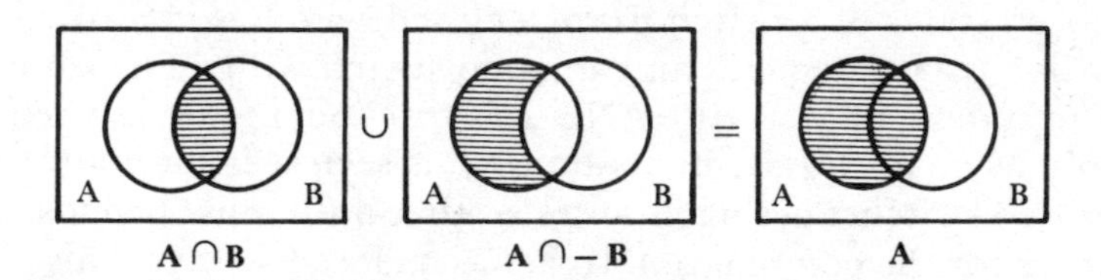

Figure 3.3. *Pictorial verification of a set theorem*

The type of diagram shown in Figure 3.3 is known as a Venn diagram. These do not constitute a formal proof of the set theorem, merely a pictorial representation of the sense of the equality. The box represents the set of all elements under consideration, say the pupils in a classroom. Set A and set B, each shown as a circle, represent, say, children who have brothers and children who have sisters, respectively. Interpreted in this way, the shaded area representing A ∩ B is the set of all children with both brothers and sisters, and so on. The theorem then says that by taking the set of children with both brothers and sisters, together with the set of those who have brothers and no sisters, one obtains the set of children who have brothers.

Clearly there is no need to validate the theorem. Its truth is a logical consequence of the definitions of sets and their operations.

Boolean algebra and switching theory

It may be of some interest to note that switching systems [ie all computers, telephone exchanges and other machines that use binary (on/off) devices] operate solely according to the laws of set theory. This is the result of the work of two people, British mathematician George Boole in 1850 and American engineer Claude Shannon in 1938. Boolean algebra, which preceded Cantor's definition of set theory by 50 years, comprises a set of laws that relates to combinations of statements that may either be true or false. This turns out to be a collection of laws that is equivalent to those of set theory. In fact, it is possible to interpret the theorem illustrated in Figure 3.3 as meaning: '(A is true AND B is true) or (A is true AND B is NOT true)' is the same as saying 'A is true'.

Claude Shannon recognized a further equivalence, and that is the resemblance of a true/false statement to the open and closed states of a switch. Here a closed switch is identified with a true statement, and an open switch with a false one. The statement 'A is true AND B is true' being true in itself only when both statements are true, is seen as being equivalent to two switches acting in series so that both must be closed in order for the combination to act as a closed switch. This means that the theorems of Boolean algebra can reflect effects in the design of switching circuits. The theorem that was pursued earlier has a significance here, as shown in Figure 3.4.

Engineers call this the *minimization theorem* and it is this which allows complex structures to be replaced by simpler ones.

Is set theory consistent?

It should be noted that this vision of a system of mathematics, totally consistent and based on Cantor's set theory, is misleading. Although it took the best part of two thousand years to recognize that Euclidean geometry was not consistent, it only took a decade or two to discover a similar pattern in set theory.

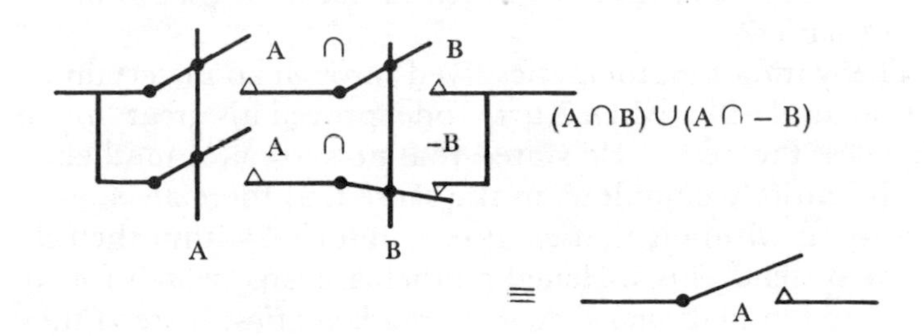

Figure 3.4. *Switching circuit minimization: illustrating the use of Boolean algebra in the design of switching circuits*

Again, as with Euclid's parallel lines notion, the intuitive idea of a set begins to falter when the notion is extended to sets of infinite sizes. This discovery was made early this century by Bertrand Russell and is now hailed as a major paradox of mathematical history. It is worth stating this here, as it is an object lesson on the misleading effect that mathematical modelling may produce, if the use of a model is extended far beyond the range within which it is known to be valid.

Russell's paradox concerns that gigantic concept known as the set of all sets, say S. This set divides into two mutually exclusive sets S1 and S2. S1 is the set of all sets that do not belong to themselves. For example, the set of cows is not a cow and therefore belongs to S1. S2 is the set of sets that do belong to themselves. For example, the 'set of things discussed in this paragraph' is in itself a thing discussed in this paragraph and therefore belongs to S2. Setting out the definition of S1 as a logical statement gives: *X belongs to S1 if and only if X does not belong to X.* This definition should hold for all sets X in S1. But what of S1 itself? Replacing X in the above definition by S1 gives: *S1 belongs to S1 if and only if S1 does not belong to S1.*

This crisp paradox serves to show that there is an inconsistency in set theory and this seriously undermines the notion that 'good' systems of mathematics are those that are totally self consistent. So, if physical measurement does not provide a validation of the excellence of mathematical models, and if systems that within themselves appear to have unquestionable mathematical validity prove to be unreliable, where does one look? How much faith can be placed in mathematics?

The world of mathematics lived through an uncertain period until 1931 when Kurt Godel proved his great 'incompleteness theorems'. He stated that no system of mathematics can be entirely complete, in the sense that there are some constructs within it that cannot be resolved within the rules of the system. This softened mathematicians' search for the ultimate foundational system of mathematics. Instead they began a more sober cataloguing of different systems with different rules.

Modern algebraic systems

Despite the swings in confidence over whether the set is the fundamental element of mathematics, pure mathematicians have concerned themselves with the classification of axiomatic systems based on sets, with ever increasing and more restrictive axioms. To illustrate this procedure, one of the simplest of these systems, one which is called a *group,* is examined here.

The objects of an algebraic system are generally defined as a set. Indeed, a group starts with a set of elements, for instance:

$$G = \{g_1, g_2, g_3 \ldots\}$$

Here it is assumed that the groups contain a finite set of elements.

Next, a single operation is defined that may be used on pairs of elements from the set G. The symbol * will be used to indicate that the operation is being performed, eg $g_1 * g_2$. Finally, the restrictions are listed on the operation that define the algebraic system, in this case the group.

The first of these restrictions is that G and * must be *closed.* That is, taking any two arbitrary elements of G, say g_1 and g_2, closure requires that $g_1 * g_2$ shall be in G. For example, if G is defined as the three integer set [1,2,3] and * as the process of addition, then closure does not hold. Whereas if G contained *all* the integers (and was thus infinite) closure could be said to hold.

The second restriction requires that for any three arbitrarily chosen elements of G, say g_1, g_2 and g_3, the following must hold:

$$g_1*(g_2*g_3) = (g_1*g_2)*g_3$$

The brackets indicate that their content represents the first application of the * operation. This is known as *association.* The reader will soon see that the system consisting of the set of all integers with the operation of addition is associative.

Thirdly, in order to have a group, an *identity* element must be found among the elements of G. This element i is defined (for all elements of G) as:

$$i*g_1 = g_1*i = g_1$$

In the system of integers and addition it is the integer 0 that acts as identity element.

Finally, a group requires that every element has an *inverse.* That is, for any arbitrarily chosen element in G (say g_1) there must be an element in G (say g_2) for which:

$$g_1*g_2 - i$$

It should be noted that if G were to consist of the set of all non-negative integers only, then G would not form a group under the operation of addition. But if the negative integers were added to G, then every element would have an inverse — its own negative integer.

An example of a group that is *finite* in the sense that G is finite, is the 12 (or 24) hour clock. For the sake of simplicity consider G as consisting of the twelve integers that represent the hours. The operation is that of simple addition. Clearly the system is *closed* as, for example, 6 + 8 = 2, etc. The identity element is 12, as 12 + 5 = 5 + 12 = 5, for example. Also every element of this system has an inverse, ie its complement of 12. For example, 7 and 5 are inverses of one another.

In the context of digital computing systems, every counter may be seen as a group. Groups are also useful in bringing together problems where permutations are important. Consider all the permutations of the letters a, b and c. These are shown on page 60.

These have been numbered from 1 to 6, and it is these numbers that constitute the elements of set G. The number 3 can be assigned to the permutation that takes abc into bac, and so on, making set G the set of all possible permutations of abc. The operation is given the meaning 'followed by'. So, 3*4 is permutation 3 followed by permutation 4. Starting with abc, 3 gives bac. Application of the transpositions indicated by 4 to bac gives acb, which is the same as applying 2 to abc in the first place, ie 3*4 = 2. The system is obviously closed and (perhaps not so obvious) associative. The identity is 1 and each element has an inverse.

a	a	b	b	c	c
b	c	a	c	a	b
c	b	c	a	b	a
1	2	3	4	5	6

It is this type of group that leads to the establishment of a link between groups and finite state machines as encountered in Chapter 2. The permutation table above bears some resemblance to the state table of Figure 2.3.

Semi-groups and finite-state automata

Consider a finite-state automaton which has a finite set of inputs, $i_1, i_2, i_3 \ldots i_n$, and a finite set of states, $s_1, s_2, s_3 \ldots s_m$. The states ordered as $(s_1, s_2, s_3 \ldots s_m)$ is the first object of a set (such as permutation 1 in the previous example). The consequence of applying a sequence of inputs is that a new object will be found corresponding to the list of states reached by the states in the first object. For example, s_1 might end in s_3 after the application of the input sequence s_2 to s_1, s_3 to s_6 and s_m to s_1 (again). This set of objects can be called q_1, q_2, etc. There is only a finite maximum number of these objects, this being precisely m^m. As in the case of the permutation group, the meaning of object q_x can be interpreted as the process of going from object q_1 to object q_x. Such a process is brought about by the application of some sequence of inputs.

Again, taking the cue from the permutation group and defining the operation * as 'followed by', $q_i * q_j$ is read as 'the application of an input sequence that takes q_1 to q_i, followed by the application of a sequence that takes q_i to q_j. Evidently, the set of objects $G = q_1, q_2 \ldots q_m$ and the operation * (as defined) is closed, since any combination of sequence pairs must lead to some element of G. Associativity may also be seen to hold as $(q_j * q_k) * q_p$ and $q_j * (q_k * q_p)$ both imply the same sums of input sequences, and hence imply the same object in G. So far, so good.

Problems arise when it becomes evident that the definition of a finite-state automaton does not provide the guarantee of an identity element. This arises because there is no guarantee that q_1 occurs as an object in the next-state table. This also removes the guarantee of the existence of inverses. (In short, we seem to have got only part of the way there.) Indeed, an algebraic system with closure and association alone is called a semi-group, and the theory of finite-state machines is synonymous with that of semi-groups. To explore some important features of this the finite-state machine shown in the state table of Figure 3.5 will now be considered.

	next state	*inputs* i_1	i_2
present state	a	a	b
	b	b	c
	c	c	a

Figure 3.5. *State table for a three-state automaton*

The way to determine all the elements of the semi-group is to consider ever longer sequences of inputs as shown below.

Let q_1 be the object abc. Consider sequences of length 1:

sequence	*resulting object*	*object name*	*comment*
i_1	abc	q_1	known
i_2	bca	q_2	new

Going on to sequences of length 2, only those starting in i_2 need be considered, as i_1 has resulted in a known object.

sequence	*resulting object*	*object name*	*comment*
$i_2 i_1$	bca	q_2	known
$i_2 i_2$	cab	q_3	new

Again, only the sequences that generate new objects need to be taken further. It has been shown previously that adding i_1 to a sequence does not generate new objects. Thus, the only length 3 sequence which could generate a new object is $i_2 i_2 i_2$:

sequence	*resulting object*	*object name*	*comment*
$i_2 i_2 i_2$	abc	q_1	known

Since there are now no new objects they must all have been found. The first noticeable feature of this procedure is that it determines all the relevant combinations of states that occur during the operation of the machine. It is quite a common occurrence that, as here, only three out of a possible 27 objects actually occur.

Having discovered that G = $\{q_1, q_2, q_3\}$ it is conventional to define, using a state table, the relationship between these elements under the defined operation *, ie:

*	q_1	q_2	q_3
q_1	q_1	q_2	q_3
q_2	q_2	q_3	q_1
q_3	q_3	q_1	q_2

Examination of this table shows that, although the procedure was started from the definition of a simple finite state machine, a group has actually been created. The identity element is q_1 and every element has an inverse. Truth tables for operations in abstract algebra are helpful in bringing to light the properties used for a classification. For example, the table shows the existence of the identity element q_1, since the first column is the same as the set of objects at the left of the table. Also, the fact that every element has an inverse is shown by the occurrence of only one identity element in each column and row. Indeed, in this particular group, the symmetry about the top-left to bottom-right diagonal indicates that for each element pair the following holds:

$$q_1 * q_2 = q_2 * q_1$$

This property is called *commutation* and what has been found here is a *commutative group.*

The reader may care to apply the above method to a slightly modified machine as shown in Figure 3.6. It should be noted that this machine has a much greater number of elements and does not qualify to be a group, but only a semi-group.

So far, the objects or elements of a semi-group resulting from a finite-state automaton, have a meaning that appears to

next state	*inputs* i_1	i_2
a	b	c
b	c	b
c	a	c

Figure 3.6. *State table for a semi-group machine*

be somewhat unrelated to the task of the finite-state machine. This impression may easily be corrected. The behaviour of the finite-state automaton depends on a particular input sequence. The complete set of input sequences, based on an input set $I = \{ i_1, i_2, i_3 \ldots i_n \}$, can be defined as:

$$I^+ = \{ i_1, i_2 \ldots i_1 i_1, i_1 i_2 \ldots i_1 i_1 i_2 i_n \ldots \}$$

Clearly this set is infinite. However, the objects q_1, q_2 and q_3 divide this set into three parts, one for each object. From the procedure that has been followed, it is not hard to identify these divisions (each of these is also infinite) as:

q_1: $\{ i_1, i_1 i_1, i_1 i_1 i_1 \ldots i_2 i_2 i_2, i_2 i_2 i_2 i_1 \ldots \}$
q_2: $\{ i_2, i_1 i_2, i_2 i_1, i_2 i_1 i_1 \ldots i_2 i_2 i_2 i_2 \ldots \}$
q_3: $\{ i_2 i_2, i_2 i_2 i_1, i_2 i_2 i_1 i_1 \ldots i_1 i_2 i_2 \ldots \}$

Thus, the objects of the semi-group represent sets of sequences that are identical in terms of the effect that they have on the machine. As such, they are fundamental parameters that describe the effect of the machine on the set of all possible sequences.

Finiteness

Associating finite-state machines with semi-groups has shown that the effect of such machines is to break up the infinite set of input strings into a finite number of sets (also infinite, set by set). Within each of these sets the machine reacts in exactly the same way. In terms of intelligence, this means that the best that this kind of machine can do is to divide its input stream into a finite number of meanings.

This will not suffice if an intelligent system is ever going to react sensibly to language. Clearly, if the words of the English language are taken as symbols input to a machine, each *meaning* must be represented by a different state within the machine so as to be distinguishable, hence the poor prospect for finite-state machines in this field. The rest of this chapter will discuss mathematical alternatives to the finite-state machine which provide models whose capacity for representing meaning is potentially infinite.

The mathematics of language

An application of mathematical modelling that belongs firmly in the latter half of this century is that of mathematical linguistics. The pioneering work of American mathematician Noam Chomsky is now central not only to the design of intelligent systems, but also to an understanding of the design of computer languages. It also provides a logical framework within which we, as humans, can begin to analyse what we mean by 'grammar' in the context of the language we use to communicate with others.

The formal definition of a language requires four sets:

V_t: a vocabulary of objects that make up the language (words);
V_n: a vocabulary of auxiliary symbols that act as instruments in assessing the grammatical validity of a sentence [examples are symbols such as (noun), (verb)];
P: a set of rules; and
S: a set containing just one symbol called the starting symbol; this is usually a member of V_n and is used to start off the process of generating legitimate sentences in the language.

In fact, this description relates to the class of languages known as *phrase structured.* It was this class that concerned Noam Chomsky. Clearly, it is possible to define languages in other ways. For example, the statement 'the language consisting of strings aa^R, where a is any string of letters and a^R is that string reversed' defines precisely the language of palendromic strings discussed in Chapter 2.

Among phrase-structured languages, there is a class that is called *context free.* The reason for this is that the production rules are all specified in the form:

A := b
where A is an element of V_n and b is any string of symbols from either V_n or V_t.

The symbol := reads 'may be replaced by'. To see how this works consider a system that generates English-like sentences.

In this system,

V_n: {(sentence), (nounphrase), (verb), (article), (noun), (intransitive verb)}
V_t: {the, a, man, cat, ball, throws, sees, sleeps}

The elements of these sets are all words in the English language. What is proposed here, however, is that the words in V_n will never appear in the sentences of the very restricted language about to be defined. It is only the limited set of eight words in V_t that will be contained in legitimate sentences. The replacement relationships among the above objects can be defined by listing P, the *production rules* of the language.

P: (sentence) := (nounphrase)(verb)(nounphrase)/(nounphrase)
(intransitive verb)(nounphrase) := (article)(noun)
(verb) := throws/sees
(article) := the/a
(noun) := man/cat/ball
(intransitive verb) := sleeps
S: (sentence)

Several points need to be made about this method of notation. First, sequences like '(article)(noun)' read '(article) *followed by*(noun)'. Second, sequences like 'the/a' read 'the *or* a'. Given these interpretations the actual sequences of the language may be generated, bearing in mind that when the oblique symbol (/) appears only one of the possible alternatives can be chosen, eg:

(sentence) := (nounphrase)(verb)(nounphrase)
:= (article)(noun)throws(article)(noun)
:= a man throws the ball

It must immediately be said that this production procedure has nothing to do with the meaning of the sentences it generates. Indeed, it is clear that quite meaningless sentences such as 'the ball sleeps' or 'the ball throws a cat' may be generated. These mathematical productions only ensure the grammatical correctness of the sentences. An approach to the checking of meaning correctness will be encountered in Chapter 4.

One of the most important discoveries that Chomsky made, in respect to context-free languages, was to show that given a definition of the language, it may not be possible to check the correctness of a given sentence by the use of a state automaton of the kind described in Chapter 2. The reason for this may be illustrated by taking the definition of another language as an example.

$$
\begin{array}{lll}
V_n & : & \{ A \} \\
V_t & : & \{ (,) \} \\
P & : & A := (A)/().
\end{array}
$$

A little patience will show that this is the language of all nested brackets of the type:

()
(())
.
.
.
((((((((((((((((((())))))))))))))))))))).
.
.
.

The way in which a machine that checks the mathematical validity of a sentence might be expected to work would involve accepting the sequence of symbols from V_t from a definite starting point. At the exhaustion of the string to be tested, the machine would provide a *pass* or *fail* output signal. Clearly, as has been shown in Chapter 2, no finite-state automaton can accept such strings. This is due not only to the fact that the string may be infinite, but is also a result of not knowing how many states may be required as the input sequence unfolds. There appears to be a need for machines that can call on additional memory as the need for more states develops.

Such a machine will now be described – this is called a *pushdown stack automaton.* It may be necessary, here, to reassure the astute reader who may be concerned about the intrusion of the descriptions of machines, in this, a chapter primarily concerned with mathematical modelling. This is quite intentional and legitimate. It has been shown earlier that there is a direct correspondence between a finite-state machine and a semi-group. This correspondence may be generalized to say that there is a direct relationship between classes of machines and classes of algebraic systems. Therefore, it is quite acceptable to talk of these mathematical models as if they were machines. After all, this is a book about the design of systems.

The 'stack' illustrated in Figure 3.7 provides the notionally infinite memory that appears to be required by this class of languages. The operation of this system may be illustrated on the language of nested brackets as follows. Assume that the sequence is presented to the machine as it might be typed, ie from left to right. The finite state machine (FSM) starts by putting successive brackets [(] on the stack. The stack in such machines is just like a stack of plates in a plate dispenser. As a symbol is put on the top, all the symbols below move down one position.

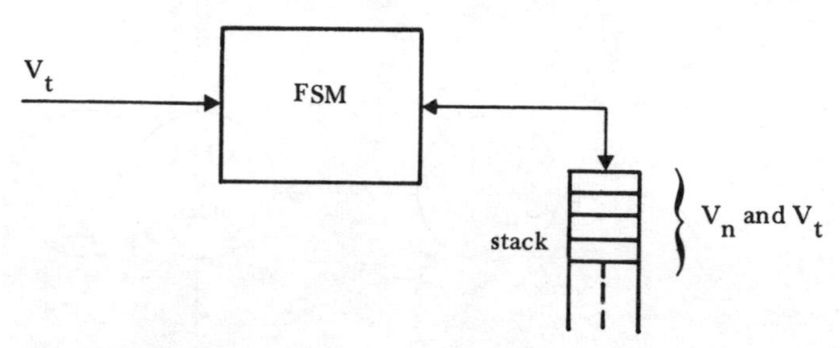

Figure 3.7. *A pushdown stack automaton – the stack refers to the additional memory which becomes available as it is required*

If the top of the stack symbol is '(' and the input symbol is ')' then the '(' on the top of the stack is removed and the contents of the stack all move up one. However, once the process of taking elements off the top of the stack has started, the appearance of a '(' symbol will cause the system to signal a failure. On the other hand, if the stack is emptied at the same time as the input string runs out of symbols, then the system signals a pass. This procedure can be illustrated by the automaton structure shown in Figure 3.8.

To tie up the action of the pushdown stack automaton with sentences such as 'a man throws the ball,' take a look at the sequence of stack states that is involved in the checking of such a sentence. This is shown over and it should be noted how the system can do its job by operating only on the top symbol of the stack. Also, the action of the FSM is merely the application of one particular production rule. However, the example does not show *how* the appropriate rule is selected. In general, the machine would have to try each appropriate rule in turn, before a sentence can be failed. This could be a lengthy procedure and has therefore been omitted from the example shown here.

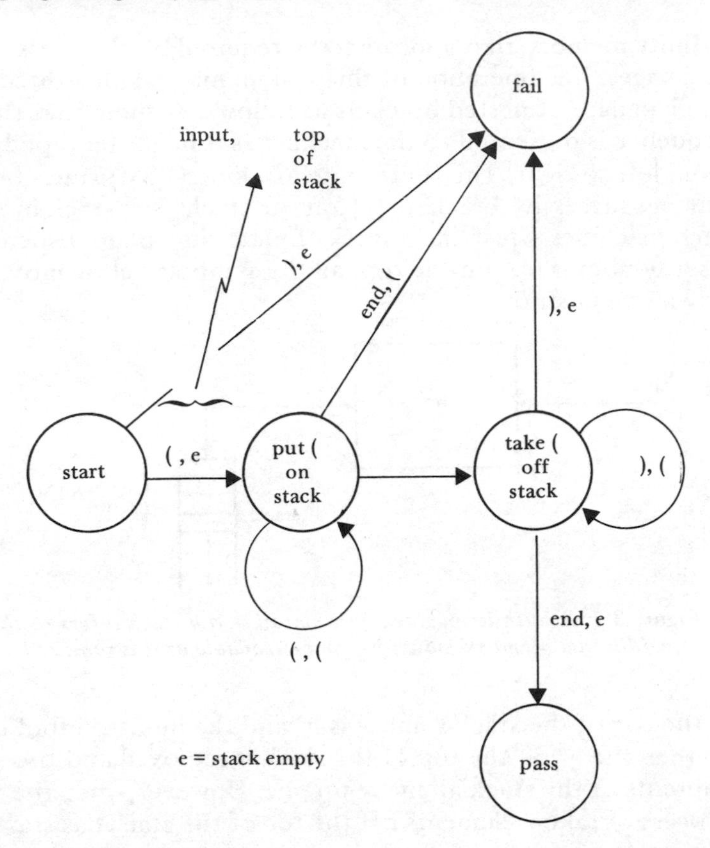

Figure 3.8. *FSM action for the pushdown stack automaton*

In principle, the machine applies production rules to the top of the stack until the top symbol matches the input symbol, at which point the latter is accepted. The system then concerns itself with the next input symbol. When the entire input string has been processed, it is passed only if the stack is empty.

input symbol	*stack content*	*comment*
a	empty	starting condition
a	(sentence)	inevitable first step
a	(nounphrase) (verb) (nounphrase)	the first of the two possible rules has been applied

input symbol	*stack content*	*comment*
a	(article) (noun) (verb) (nounphrase)	(nounphrase) has been replaced in the only possible way
a	a (noun) (verb) (nounphrase)	(article) replaced by 'a'
man	(noun) (verb) (nounphrase)	'a' has been accepted and the next symbol is input
man	man (verb) (nounphrase)	(noun) has been replaced by 'man'
throws	(verb) (nounphrase)	'man' has been accepted
throws	throws (nounphrase)	(verb) replaced by 'throws'
the	(nounphrase)	'throws' accepted
the	(article) (noun)	(nounphrase) replaced
the	the (noun)	(article) replaced
ball	(noun)	'the' accepted
ball	ball	(noun) replaced
end of string	empty stack	entire sentence accepted

Turing machines

The pushdown stack automaton shown in Figure 3.7 bears a resemblance to a much older mathematical idea due to Alan Turing. He was a British mathematician who was concerned with the process of computation much before the digital computer had been invented.

This neatly illustrates the point that machines are mathematical objects, as Turing was concerned only with the mathematical meaning of computation. His concept is illustrated in Figure 3.9, where it should be noted that the need for an infinite memory is provided by the concept of an infinite tape. An FSM is capable of moving backwards and forwards over this tape, and of both reading symbols from it and replacing them by other symbols.

The problem of checking nested brackets could be carried out using this machine. The process starts with the string to be tested printed on adjacent locations on the tape. The rest of the tape is blank. The FSM would simply move backwards and forwards over the tape replacing the brackets at the outer edges of the string by blanks only if such pairs match. The result must be an empty tape (within the area of the string) or else the string is not correct.

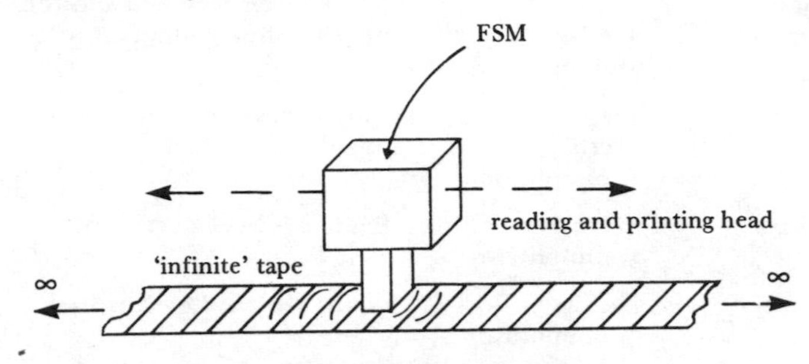

Figure 3.9. *A Turing machine*

Turing's great contribution to mathematics was not so much the invention of this rather impractical machine, but the proof of a theorem which showed that the set of mathematical tasks that is *computable,* is precisely the same as the set that can be executed using the machine.

Summary

Intelligent systems are generally referred to as systems that compute, or transform information. The central message in this chapter is that this process has a sound foundation in modern mathematics.

In the first part of the chapter it was shown that this type of mathematics is distinguished by its self-consistency. It was then shown that some of the fundamental systems within modern mathematics, ie set theory and group theory, have a close affinity with computational machines. The final part of the chapter turned the tables on this issue and showed that it is possible to 'do' mathematics by thinking about abstract machines. This is of particular importance in new areas of mathematics such as the analysis of grammar and language.

A universal computing machine has been described – the Turing machine. This can be used in discussing the concept of computable and non-computable functions. However, the theory does not say *how* a task may be computed, eg the method suggested for checking nested brackets. Such methods are known as 'algorithms' and these are the subject of Chapter 4.

CHAPTER 4

Algorithmic models in artificial intelligence

The word 'algorithm' only entered the *Oxford Dictionary* in 1976, although, by then, it had been a word much used by computer programmers for some 20 years. The root of the word is the same as that for 'arithmetic', deriving from the name of a ninth century Egyptian mathematician, Al-Kuwarizmi. In the days when the arithmetic powers of the computer were thought to be its main strength, the word came into use in the sense of 'doing things with numbers'. Now it may be loosely interpreted as meaning 'a way of doing things on a computer'.

An algorithm should not be confused with a program. For example, part of an algorithm may be stated as:

> 'Whenever variable P is other than 0, variable Q must be set to 1 before the rest of the algorithm can proceed.'

If written in the computer language BASIC this becomes a program:

```
200 if P ≠ ∅ then Q = 1
300 . . .
```

Similarly, a PASCAL program for the same algorithm is:

```
if P ≠ ∅ then
q:=1
. . .
```

An algorithm, therefore, is a statement written with computational precision of how things should be done. A program is an encoding of the algorithm into a computer language that can be executed using a particular computer. From the point of view of this chapter, the interest in algorithms centres on their precision and their independence from programming. Their precision is used to create models of 'intelligent' systems which, given a proper encoding into a program, can then be expected to run on any computer.

Algorithmic models of intelligent systems are called *artificial intelligence.* A broad definition often used in this context is: 'Artificial intelligence concerns itself with algorithms which, when run on a computer, cause the computer to perform acts which, if done by humans, would be said to be intelligent.'

Since the original development of artificial intelligence in the late 1950s, several researchers have argued that the algorithms have something to say about the way that real intelligence is organized in humans. Much of this way of thinking has now been dispelled, and artificial intelligence algorithms are now seen as interesting models of the way complex tasks may be organized on a computer. A most sobering quote on the subject may be found in Nils Nilsson's book, *Principles of Artificial Intelligence*: 'If ... a science of intelligence could be developed, it could guide the design of intelligent machines as well as explicate intelligent behaviour as it occurs in humans and other animals. Since the development of such a theory is still very much a goal rather than an accomplishment of artificial intelligence, we limit our attention here to those principles that are relevant to the engineering goal of building intelligent machines.'

This is precisely the view taken in this book. There is much engineering excellence in the algorithmic models that have been devised to make a computer behave intelligently in its own right.

There are four such major areas of 'intelligent' human activity that have come under the scrutiny of workers in artificial intelligence: game playing, problem solving, artificial vision – including pattern recognition – and natural language understanding. Simple examples of the algorithmic models involved in each of these activities will now be considered.

Game playing

Not only is this an interesting area of human intelligence, but also, in its machine form, it has been developed into a commercial activity of some magnitude. Chess-playing machines have had such a large impact on the leisure market as to lead silicon chip manufacturers to design special chess-playing chips. Such chips embody many of the characteristics of the algorithms under discussion here. Such activity has also given rise to a new game, that of computer chess, which is now played in some major international tournaments. However, it should be stressed that winners of such tournaments are not the computers themselves but their programmers, whose skill at writing algorithms is the topic under considcration.

Two major algorithmic approaches will be considered here, each of which is commonly used to make computer game-playing more efficient. Before doing so a game will be described that, rather than being rivetingly exciting to play, facilitates the explanation of the algorithms. The game is called the *Digi-Munch Game* and is played on a 4 x 4 matrix with two tokens placed as shown in Figure 4.1.

1	5	13	14
2	Y	8	12
7	3	X	10
6	9	11	4

Figure 4.1. *Layout of the board at the start of the Digi-Munch Game*

The tokens, labelled X and Y, are placed at random on the board and are used by two players, respectively. The numbers 1 to 14 are then arbitrarily placed on the board. The players then take turns to move their token to one of four possible edge-neighbour cells (diagonal moves are not allowed). On moving, the player collects the points indicated in the square, and reduces the value of that square to zero. Moves are permitted only to squares with non-zero values. If, at any point, a player moves into the square occupied by his opponent, the game is ended and the total scores are counted. The game is also ended if all the numbers are used or an impasse has been reached. X starts, and here we shall assume that X, played by a machine, is playing Y, a human opponent.

Clearly, both the human and the machine need to 'think' several steps ahead, in order to decide on their next move. The first algorithmic model seeks to represent this type of thinking. It is called the *minimax algorithm* and operates on the basis that, at alternative levels of looking ahead the player must try to maximize his advantage, while at the intervening levels his opponent will try to minimize it.

The algorithm starts with a decision that the machine will look *N* levels ahead, and that it is capable of calculating all the possible advantages and disadvantages of the various states of the game that might have been reached at that point. To follow through this process of evaluation with Digi-Munch, assume that the machine starts and looks three moves ahead.

First move (X), possible moves and scores:
8,10,11,3

Second move (Y), possible moves (each of the nested brackets is related to the first move of X, in the order shown):
(5,0,3,2)(5,8,3,2)(5,8,3,2)(5,8,0,2)

The advantage for X can now be related to these moves by deducting Y's score from that of X in the first round. Hence, the scores are:
(3,*8*,5,6)(5,2,7,8)(6,3,8,9)(–2,–1,*3*,1)
The scores printed in italic type are end-of-game scores showing a win for X as they are positive. Negative values would indicate wins for Y. However, it will be shown later that Y would avoid taking such deliberately suicidal moves.

Third move (X), possible moves [again nested brackets are used to indicate the relation to previous moves, (X) indicating a win for X at the previous level, but included for completeness]:
((13,12)(X)(13,12)(13,12))((12, 4)(12, 4)(12, 4)(12, 4))
((9,4)(9,4)(9,4)(9,4))((7,9)(7,9) (X) (7,9))

The scores may be derived from these moves by adding the third move values to the cumulative totals already in hand for X, so:
((16,15) (X) (18,17)(19,18))((17,9)(14,6)(19,11)(20,12))
((15,10)(12, 7)(17,12)(18,13))((5,7)(2,4) (X) (8,10))

The minimax algorithm actually starts with this last list, called list-3. It is assumed that if *n* in list-*n* is odd, X, in its previous move, will select moves within the inner brackets which maximize its advantage. On the other hand, if *n* is even, Y will choose a move within the inner brackets that minimizes X's advantage. Working backwards from level N it is possible to predict all the likely moves, including the next move that needs to be taken by X at the actual point in the game. Applying this rule to level-3 (which is odd), the scores that are maximum within the inner brackets are chosen giving a level-2 list, in which the inner brackets have been removed, as shown below:

(16,X,18,19)(17,14,19,20)(15,12,17,18)(7,4,X,10)

This is known as the process of *backing up,* which may be continued to back scores up to the level-1 values, using the minimal inner brackets choice now, because level-2 is odd. Thus, the level-1 scores are 16,14,12,4.

This now corresponds to the north,east,south and west moves of X at its next move. Clearly, the north move leads to the best advantage for X at the third level and should therefore be taken. It is interesting to note that if X had looked only one step ahead, it would have chosen the south move. Equally, were X to look even further ahead, it may be led to other choices at level-1. The minimax algorithm can be succinctly summarized as:

> Given a level-n list, back up to the level $(n-1)$ list by replacing the inner brackets by their maximum value, if n is odd and their minimum value, if n is even. At level-1 take the move indicated by the maximum score.

An immediate question arises regarding the applicability of this algorithm to games that do not have as obvious a point-scoring scheme as Digi-Munch. The answer holds few surprises: it is up to the programmer to invent a way of evaluating board positions. Indeed, it is here that the skill of the programmer becomes embedded in his program, and could well determine its quality. In chess, for example, board patterns may be given points as follows:

Checkmate	=	1000 points
Queen – King fork	=	100 points
Queen – Rook skewer	=	50 points
Queen threat	=	15 points

In one of the earliest game-playing programs, built by A L Samuel in 1959, these points were learnt by the system and improved as it gained experience. It is current practice, however, to avoid possibly long learning runs by building-in the desired evaluations.

The difficulty with most games is that in order to play a reasonable game, the system must look many levels ahead. The list of scores tends to grow alarmingly under such conditions, and prohibitively long delays may occur, even with very fast machines. To combat this use is made of another important algorithm, the *alpha-beta* scheme. This still uses the minimax principle, but takes short cuts when certain searches are expected to be futile. The central idea of the scheme is to carry out a partial *depth-first* search so as to discover some bounds that are likely not to be breached in the search for good moves. For example, if a win is discovered against the most powerful play of the opponent in a depth-first evaluation of moves, it will not be necessary to search all of the possibilities, as a winning strategy has been found. The alpha-beta method, however, does not only look for wins, but applies the same principle to all moves whose excellence it calculates cannot be exceeded.

A depth-first search to level-3 would mean that the evaluation of the score would be assessed in sequence, say, from left to right. Instead of using the greek letters alpha and beta (from which the algorithm derives its name) the letters a and b shall be used; a is used to identify the odd (maximizing) brackets in a score list, while b identifies the even (minimizing) ones. Subscripts are used to identify a particular bracket at a particular level, eg a_{32} indicates the second bracket at the third level.

Taking the level-3 score list as it might be evaluated from left to right, this would be labelled as:

```
  (  (16,15) (. . .
b21a31     a32
```

Clearly bracket a_{31} will evaluate to 16, which can be taken as a temporary value for b_{21}. As the rest of the bracket (b_{21}) comes in:

```
(16(X)(18,17)(19,18))
b21
```

a glance shows that this value of 16 cannot be undercut, and that therefore 16 becomes the permanent value of b_{21}. It should be noted that some computation has been saved, since it has not been necessary to carry out the process of maximizing. So far, therefore, the evaluation can be summarized as follows:

((16)((17,9) (14,6) (. . .
$a_{11}b_{21}\ b_{22}\ a_{35}\quad a_{36}\quad a_{37}$

Here a_{36} will give b_{22} a value of, at most, 14, which cannot be exceeded whatever happens in a_{37} and a_{38}. Thus, any calculation in b_{22} beyond a_{36} may be discontinued as its value will never exceed that of b_{21} which, so far, dominates a_{11}. It is easy to confirm that in b_{23} and b_{24} only the first inner a bracket need be evaluated to show that b_{21} remains dominant.

On average, this algorithm saves about 40% of computational effort in most game-playing applications, despite the fact that the savings are somewhat haphazard as they depend on the order in which the evaluation is made.

Problem solving

There is a similarity between problem solving and game playing, in the sense that the solution of a problem can be represented as a progression between the starting conditions and a solution through sets of states. To reach and consume a banana (solution state) a monkey has to work out the intermediate state of picking up and using a stick.

The difficulty with many general classes of problem is that it is difficult to find a suitable way of measuring how far from a goal the intermediate states of a solution might be. Clearly, this is not true of all problems. Say the problem is one of getting from A to B by various means of transport, then the distance from B may be a good way of evaluating the intermediate states. In such cases it is quite possible to use the searching methods discussed in the previous section. Here we shall concentrate on those situations where such an evaluation cannot be found. We shall also try to concentrate on the general principles of problem-solving algorithms, even though the explanatory vehicle shall be a well-known puzzle: that of the cannibals and missionaries. This goes as follows.

There are three cannibals and three missionaries on the left bank of a river. They must cross to the right in a little boat that can only carry two people. Although otherwise well-behaved, the cannibals cannot be allowed to outnumber the missionaries on either bank, otherwise their natural appetites may be revived resulting in the loss of a few missionaries.

What is the shortest number of boat trips that will achieve the transfer?

The first step is to determine a way of *representing* a state of the problem. Here, a simple list can be used which shows the initial and final states of the problem:

initial state: (MMMCCC/-/1)
final state: (-/MMMCCC/r)

This notation contains three fields: one for the left bank, one for the right bank and the third for the position of the boat: l for left and r for right.

The next general step is to define the complete *set of rules* whereby a transition between one state and another may be achieved. In this case there are ten rules corresponding to the possible contents of the boat and the starting bank for the boat. Explicitly, these are:

(MMl)(MCl)(CCl)(Ml)(Cl)(MMr)(MCr)(CCr)(Mr)(Cr).

Not all rules may be applied to all states. Therefore, as the third general step a *precondition list* is created which defines the applicability of each rule. It is this step that guarantees that the constraints of the problem are entered into the algorithm. A few examples follow. For rule (MMl) the precondition list is:

(MMMC/CC/l) or (MM/CCC/l).

Note that this excludes states such as (MMCC/MC/l) as they would contravene the 'outnumbered' rule. On the other hand, a rule such as (Cr) has a much wider applicability:

(MMMCC/C/r) or (MMMC/CC/r) or (MMM/CCC/r) or (MMCC/MC/r) ..., etc.

As the fourth step, a *delete list* and an *add list* are defined which specify precisely how the state will be modified when the rule is applied. For example, the delete list for rule (MMl) is (MM/-/l), while the add list for it is (-/MM/r). A computer can then easily be instructed to apply rule (MMl) to, say, (MMMC/CC/l). Having checked and passed the precondition list, it applies the delete list yielding (MC/CC/-), then the add list, yielding (MC/MMCC/r).

The final part of the algorithm is the control of the search process. This starts with the initial state and selects all the rules that contain this state in their precondition list. The rules are applied through the mechanism of the add and delete lists, generating a new set of states. In this new set, any state that has previously occurred or which is duplicated within the set is removed. The set is scrutinized to see whether it contains the target state. If it does, the process ends.

The solution to the puzzle can be illustrated by applying the algorithm:

Initial state: (MMMCCC/-/l)
Applicable rules: (MCl) (CCl) (Cl)
New states: (MMCC/MC/r), (MMMC/CC/r), (MMMCC/C/r)
Rules: (MCr) (CCr) (Cr)
(Mr) (Cr)
New states (not showing those that are removed due to duplication): (MMMCC/C/l)
Rules that do not lead to duplication: (CCl)
State: (MMM/CCC/r)
Rule: (Cr)
State: (MMMC/CC/l)
Rule: (MMl)
State: (MC/MMCC/r)
Rule: (MCr)
State: (MMCC/MC/l)
Rule: (MMl)
State: (CC/MMMC/r)
Rule: (Cr)
State: (CCC/MMM/l)
Rule: (CCl)
State: (C/MMMCC/r)
Rule: (Cr)
State: (CC/MMMC/l)
Rule: (CCl)
State: (-/MMMCCC/r) *target achieved!*

In some ways this is a fortuitous problem since the number of applicable rules becomes small, as does the number of states, as the solution advances. This need not generally be true. To help matters in situations where the number of states increases a great deal, it is possible to work both forward from the starting state and backward from the target state. In such an algorithm the two sets of states generated by the forward and backward deductions are checked for *overlap*. Overlap is an indication that a trajectory between start and end state has been found.

Artificial vision

Much of human intelligence is deeply embedded in the way that an individual makes sense of his sensory information. For the artificial intelligence enthusiast vision is probably the most tantalizing of the senses, as humans depend on it so much. It is for this reason that much effort has gone into developing algorithms that describe simple scenes. This subject is vast and here an introduction will be made of only some of the fundamental algorithms that have been used in this context. It is easiest to ignore the massive amount of computing that needs to be done in order to transform a real scene, as picked up by a television camera, say, into manageable units. Assume that a real scene has been transformed into a binary picture as shown in Figure 4.2.

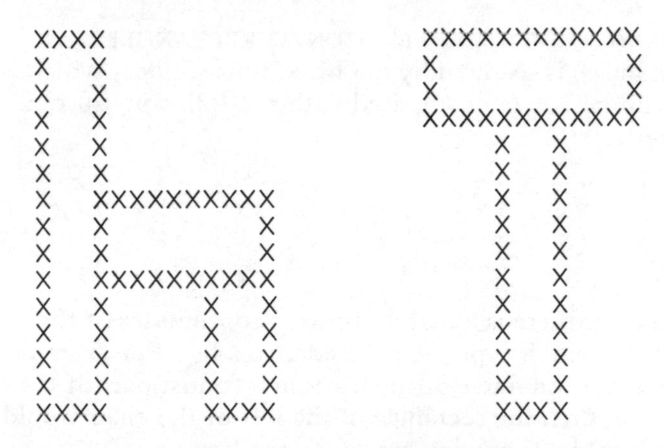

Figure 4.2. *A binary image representing a table and chair*

It is assumed that this simple image of 0s and 1s (the 1s are represented by X in Figure 4.2) is stored in memory at the beginning of the algorithm. The object of the exercise is to develop an algorithm that will process this information and generate a statement such as: 'There is a chair to the left of a table.'

The feasibility of having language-like interactions with a machine will be considered later. Of interest here is the algorithm that separates out the elements of the image, so as to make the linguistic description possible. Again it is the breaking up of the task into steps that is important. This might need to be done in situations where the images are more complex, even if the task itself may seem a little trivial.

FIRST STEP: THE NEED TO BUILD KNOWLEDGE INTO THE SYSTEM

Most vision algorithms start with an assumption about the constraints placed on the images that may be viewed. The restriction here is that any object in the field of view shall be represented in memory as a collection of vertical or horizontal rectangles of unspecified size. In much of the early work in artificial intelligence it was commonly assumed that the stored images would be two-dimensional projections of three-dimensional flat-sided objects (polyhedra). In the present example it is assumed that only the edges of these projections are stored.

SECOND STEP: IDENTIFICATION OF RECTANGLES

The image is scanned by a 3-bit x 3-bit window which is continually being compared with the following stored templates:

```
...   ...   .X.   .X.   .X.   .X.   ...   .X.
.XX   XX.   XX.   .XX   .XX   XX.   XXX   XXX
.X.   .X.   ...   ...   .X.   .X.   .X.   ...
C1    C2    C3    C4    T1    T2    T3    T4
```

Wherever there is a match, the x,y coordinates of the match and the match type are entered into a list. For example, if the x,y coordinates of the bottom leftmost part of the chair are 0,0, then the rectangle at the left of the chair would result in the following entries to the list:

C_1 at 0,22, C_2 at 4,22, C_3 at 4,0, C_4 at 0,0 . . .

Rectangles may then be found by searching down the list for groupings of four features in which two pairs of coordinates match, as in the group of four above. Clearly it is necessary to include T features in these searches, and use them in the pairing procedure. Having grouped the features into mutually exclusive sets, each representing a rectangle, these sets are then numbered, and by fitting the features back into the original image stored in the memory, rectangle labels may be added as shown in Figure 4.3.

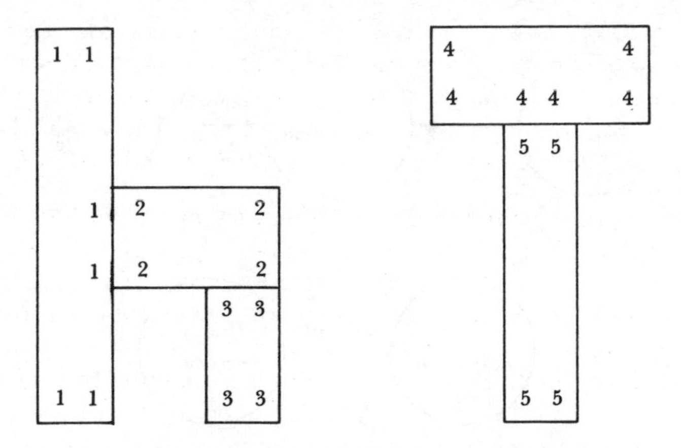

Figure 4.3. *An image of the table and chair incorporating feature labels*

The final objective in the identification of rectangles is an assessment of whether they are horizontal or vertical. All the necessary data for this is stored in the feature list, which after the process of labelling, may be partitioned into five groups, one for each rectangle in the image. It is then an easy matter to decide whether a rectangle is larger in the x or the y axis, and hence determine whether it is horizontal or vertical.

THIRD STEP: RELATIONS BETWEEN RECTANGLES

In the original features list there is sufficient information to note that the two T_1 type features between rectangle 2 and rectangle 1 are collinear with the C_2 and C_3 features in rectangle 1. It is this property that enables one to decide that rectangle 2 'abuts' on to rectangle 1. Similarly, the relationship 'supports' may be identified between 3 and 2, as well as between 5 and 4. This results in a much collapsed data structure within the machine, which simply states the nature of groups of rectangles and relations between them. Such a structure is called a *semantic network* and an illustration for the present example is presented in Figure 4.4.

The major property of such semantic networks is that they are invariant to seemingly irrelevant details of the image. For example, the same semantic network would arise, were the sizes of the rectangles altered slightly.

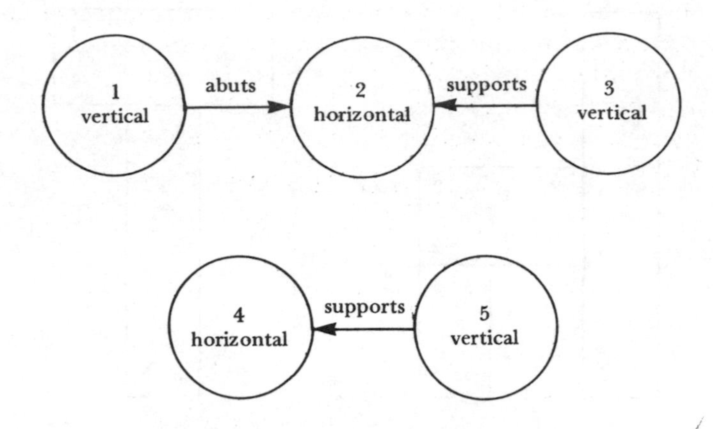

Figure 4.4. *A semantic network derived from the image of the table and chair shown in Figure 4.3*

FOURTH STEP: THE ASSIGNMENT OF MEANING

As yet, the algorithm has not been provided with a means for identifying a particular semantic network. This is done by a process of training, where single objects are introduced to the system, together with an appropriate label. This simply adds an extra element to the semantic network – as shown in Figure 4.5. It is this element that forms the association between the semantic network and its meaning. For example, a search through the semantic networks in memory may be initiated by the semantic network that has been derived from an unknown image. This would try to find a match with the non-label part of the networks, and when a match is found, output the associated label.

Unfortunately, if the process were based on the showing of one example only, its power of generalization would be far too broad – this is a case of *over-generalization.* For example, it would derive the chair and table meaning from a scene such as shown in Figure 4.6.

It is for this reason that the training procedure must consist not only of positive examples of objects, but also of negative ones, or 'near misses'. For example, the objects shown in Figure 4.6 could be used as near misses for chair and table.

The implication of this on the structure of the algorithm is that subtler forms of relationship labelling must be found.

For example, the link between 1 and 2 might read something like 'abuts, but not on ends', whereas the link between 2 and 3 would be 'supports end of'. The only computational demand here is that such subtleties must be derived from the geometry of the rectangles, and again this can be done from the feature list.

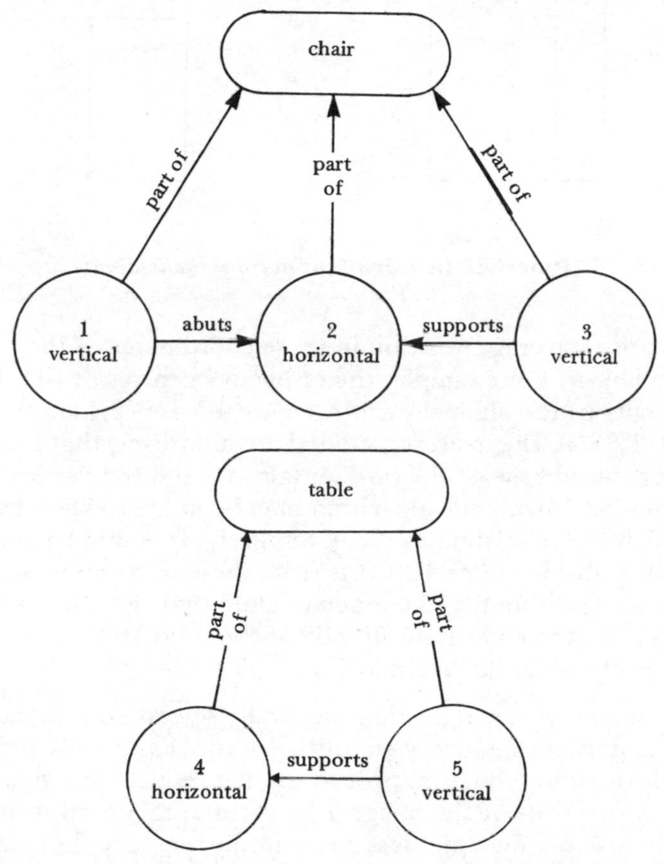

Figure 4.5. *A labelled semantic network for the table and chair shown in Figure 4.3.*

FIFTH STEP: SPATIAL RELATIONSHIPS BETWEEN OBJECTS

In order for the system to 'understand' or pronounce phrases such as 'to the left of' or '... above ...', there must be an end portion of the algorithm that calculates the truth of such statements. Once again this is based on the stored x,y positions of the features. It is therefore quite possible to

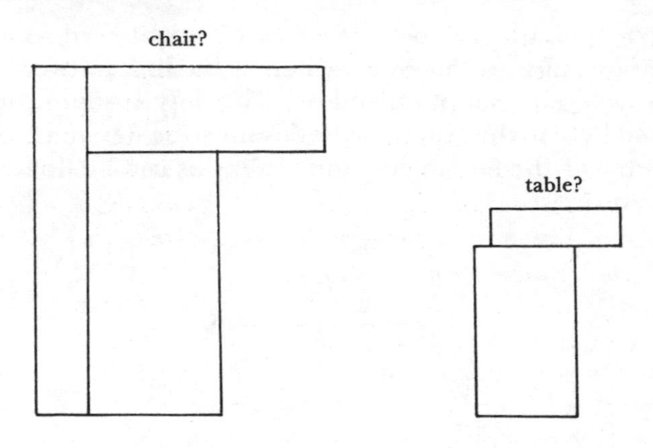

Figure 4.6. *An example of over-generalization*

calculate an average position in these coordinates of the entire object. For example, the respective centres of the three rectangles of the chair shown in Figure 4.2 are (2,11), (9,8) and (11,3) (to the nearest rounded-down integer, that is). Taking the average of the horizontals as 7 and the verticals as 7 (rounded down), the algorithm may be made to state that the chair is at coordinates (7,7). Similarly, it would be stated that the table is at (21,10). It is from these measurements that the algorithm may be made to state that the table is to the right of the chair (and slightly above it, as far as the centres of area are concerned).

In summary, vision algorithms generally operate on a clean representation of a highly simplified scene. Essentially it is an information reduction procedure that reduces the very many stored bits of the image into a structural description, which not only occupies less space in the memory, but also is sufficiently general to relate to many distortions and variations at the bit level.

Pattern recognition

There is a clear distinction between artificial vision and pattern recognition in terms of what these two fields of endeavour attempt to achieve. It has been seen that artificial vision schemes handle the structural properties of an idealized image, whereas pattern recognition is concerned much more with processing real images. A pattern recognition algorithm does not usually have the logical power of deducing relationships between objects, and is concerned primarily with the identification of simple objects, but from the raw input image. Ideally, pattern recognition algorithms complement artificial vision algorithms — for instance, they could be used to produce feature labels from raw images, as described in the previous section.

A large number of methodologies and algorithms, some of considerable mathematical sophistication, have been used during the development of pattern recognition. A method that has been seen to work well in practice is the *n-tuple method* of recognition. A particular characteristic of this method is that it is adaptive. This means that the algorithm itself has a modifiable component that can be adjusted during a *training period,* when images together with their classifications are introduced to the system. This information can then be used in subsequent recognition procedures.

Imagine that a 4-bit x 4-bit binary window is used. As an example, let us say that nut-like and bolt-like images are to be distinguished. These consist of the sets shown below, which include displaced versions of the originals.

```
XXXX   XXX•   •XXX   ••••   •XX•
•XX•   XX••   ••XX   XXXX   •XX•
•XX•   XX••   ••XX   •XX•   •XX•
•XX•   XX••   ••XX   •XX•   ••••
```

bolt-like shapes

```
•XX•   ••XX   XX••   ••••   X••X
X••X   •X••   ••X•   •XX•   X••X
X••X   •X••   ••X•   X••X   •XX•
•XX•   ••XX   XX••   X••X   ••••
```

nut-like shapes

The *n*-tuple algorithm starts with the partitioning of the field of view into groups of bits each *n* in number. (Hence the name of the algorithm.) In general, such groups are selected at random as no assumptions can be made regarding the optimal placement of such a choice. In this example assume that the field is partitioned into four squares, each of four bits. Each such *n*-tuple can therefore have 16 states. The training part of the algorithm deals with labelling those states that have occurred, in terms of their originating object. It is possible to invent a code for this: 10 for bolt and 01 for nut. This scheme allows 00 to be interpreted as *neither* and 11 as *both*.

In the table below, the result of this labelling process is shown as a result of training the system on both of the above sets of five images each. It has been assumed that the *n*-tuple areas are as follows: 1 top left, 2 top right, 3 bottom left, 4 bottom right.

state		*area number* 1	2	3	4
1	·· ··	00	00	10	10
2	·· ·X	01	00	00	00
3	·· X·	00	01	00	00
4	·· XX	10	10	01	01
5	·X ··	10	00	11	00
6	·X ·X	10	01	10	01
7	·X X·	01	00	00	01
8	·X XX	00	00	00	00
9	X· ··	00	00	00	11
10	X· ·X	00	01	01	00
11	X· X·	01	10	01	10
12	X· XX	00	00	00	00
13	XX ··	01	01	00	00
14	XX ·X	10	00	00	00
15	XX X·	00	10	00	00
16	XX XX	10	10	10	10

Figure 4.7. *The n-tuple labelling matrix for the recognition of nuts and bolts*

A scoring system is used when objects are to be identified in this table. For a given input image the number of n-tuples that score a 1 for each of the two object classes are counted, assigning the decision to the greater of the two. For example, were the first nut shape presented to the system, this contains features 14, 15,6 and 11 in areas 1,2,3 and 4, respectively. The table shows 10 for each of these four entries, giving the nut a score of 4 out of 4 and the bolt 0 out of 4 – it is correctly identified as a nut.

It should be stressed that this algorithm holds not only for two classes of object, but for as many as required (bearing in mind that the table will contain as many binary digits as there are classes). It is now possible to illustrate one of the main strengths of this algorithm, that of *generalization.* This is the property of being able to recognize an object not originally included in the training set, but similar in outline to one in that set. This is particularly important because image transducers are subject to spurious effects such as camera noise and camera vibration. Consider the image of a prototype nut whose bits on the diagonal have been corrupted through camera noise:

XXX•
•X••
••X•
X•X•

The table shows that for the n-tuple states 14, 9, 4 and 11 the responses would be 10, 00, 01 and 10. This gives a score of 2/4 for the nut and 1/4 for the bolt. The system could be thought of as saying: 'I am not too sure about this but if pressed to make a decision I would say it's a nut.' In other words, the algorithm is not only capable of generalization, but also of stating, from the strength of these responses, the confidence with which the decision is made.

It is worth enquiring what effect the choice of n in the size of the n-tuple has on the performance of the system. First, consider an n-tuple size 16 (ie one area only: precisely the entire window). This would give a prohibitively large matrix, ie one area with 65,536 states. Also, such a system would behave as a perfect memory and have no powers of generalization at all. At the other end of the scale there could be 16 areas of one bit each. The size of the matrix would be 2 x 16, but its generalization would lead to confusion in pattern detection. Indeed, after training using the same images as before, every point on the matrix will have been trained on both a 0 and a 1 so that a response of 16/16 would be generated whatever the shape of the input pattern.

So, accepting the fact that the size of the labelling matrix increases alarmingly with the value of *n*, it is the designer's job to select the value of *n* which will best provide a balance between generalization and discrimination without requiring too much memory.

One of the major advantages of this algorithm is that it is easily implemented in hardware and can be processed at very high speeds of operation. The bits in the *n*-tuple are fed simultaneously to the address terminals of as many RAMs as are required to cover the input image. It is the code of the labelling matrix that is stored in memory. This principle has been used in the design of the WISARD system at Brunel University, which recognizes images on windows of 512 x 512 bits with an *n*-tuple of 8 (ie 32,768 areas) in about 1/10th of a second.

Natural language understanding

Until the late 1960s the possibility of near-natural conversations with machines seemed most unlikely. From the point of view of algorithmic modelling the central difficulty seemed to be the intractability of semantics. Terry Winograd at the Massachusetts Institute of Technology was the first to suggest a solution, by noting that conversations whether with machines or humans have to be *about* something. He suggested that the conversation be about a restricted world, eg a robot programmed to manipulate a finite number of recognizable objects in its working area. Further, he used an idea first suggested by Chomsky, that the extraction of meaning may be guided by a process of grammatical parsing.

The example under consideration here relates to near-language conversations that may ensue when a computational system controlling a vision-based robot manipulator has a vision input such as described in the previous section. Assume that a group of nuts and bolts is in the field of view, a conversation may ensue as follows:

USER: 'Where is the small bolt?'
MACHINE: 'It is at (x,y)=(3,4), orientation = –45°.'
USER: 'Pick up the bolt.'
MACHINE: 'Which one? At (5,2) or (3,4)?'
USER: 'Pick up the small bolt.'
MACHINE: 'OK.'

Clearly the first step of the algorithm is to create a database that contains all the measured information in the input. This may be achieved by scanning over the scene through a recognition window and signalling successful identifications of objects to the database. It is possible to use the n-tuple window algorithm not only to detect the object class, but, by means of a longer code word in the labelling matrix, the orientation of an object (such as a bolt) may also be recognized. Clearly, this may not be necessary for rounded objects, and here it is assumed that the orientation of nuts is not important but that the size needs to be estimated as *large* or *small* for both objects. This too can be done by appropriate training and a further extension of the code word.

At the end of a scan the recognizer might have created the following table in the memory of the computer. This is the database that will be taken as the subject of the linguistic interaction.

number	*x position*	*y position*	*size*	*object*	*orientation*
1	1.5	1.5	large	nut	–
2	5.0	2.0	large	bolt	90°
3	3.0	4.0	small	bolt	45°
4	1.5	5.5	small	nut	–
5	6.0	5.5	large	nut	–

The way in which such databases are used is by a process of scanning against given data. For example, if the input to the database is 'large nut' it will return all the data relevant to items 1 and 5. While as sparse an input as '45°' would return uniquely, all the data associated with item 3.

Chomsky's suggestion that semantic evaluation can be guided by syntactic parsing implies the existence of a grammar such as discussed in Chapter 4. The following grammar may suit the present example:

(sentence) := (question)/(assertion)/(command)
(question) := Is (nounphrase) (relation) (nounphrase)?/
Is there (nounphrase)?/Where is (nounphrase)?
(assertion) := (nounphrase) is (relation) (nounphrase)

(command)	:=	Pick up (nounphrase)/Pick up(nounphrase) (relation)(nounphrase)
(nounphrase)	:=	(article)(noun)/(article)(adjective)(noun)
(relation)	:=	above/below/to the left of/to the right of/. . .
(article)	:=	the/a
(noun)	:=	nut/bolt
(adjective)	:=	large/small

The next part of the language-understanding algorithm consists of a specification for extractions from the database implied by the elements of the language. First, (adjective) and (noun) are set generation symbols as follows:

nut brings about the creation of set $\{1,4,5\}$ as a result of the extraction.
Similarly:
bolt results in $\{2,3\}$
large results in $\{1,2,5\}$ and
small results in $\{3,4\}$.

The stringing together of an adjective and a noun in a nounphrase becomes equivalent to the set operation of disjunction ('and-ing'). So, *small nut* results in $\{2,3\} \cap \{3,4\} = \{3\}$. Relations imply geometrical operations which also result in sets. For example, *to the left of* $\{5\}$ is the set of all objects for which the value of x is less than that of object 5. This results in $\{1,2,3,4\}$.

Consider the sentence: 'Where is the small bolt?' This parses as:

Where is (article)(adjective)(noun)?
Where is (nounphrase)?
(question)
(sentence).

As usual, the arrival at the symbol (sentence) is proof of the fact that the grammar is correct. Now it is possible to see how the parsing steps relate to the implied meaning of the sentence. Going through the parse again, but this time carrying out the set operations gives:

'Where is the small bolt?'
Where is (article) $\{3,4\} \cap \{1,4,5\}$?
Where is 4?
(question),
requiring an output about the position of a single object. This

last step goes beyond the set extraction procedures, showing that meaning can be directly attached to the type of sentence arising through the process of grammatical parsing. For example, the assertion demands a machine output which says 'true' or 'false', whereas a command implies a certain action of the robot. For example, consider again the sentence: 'Pick up the bolt.' This translates as follows:

Pick up { 2,3 }
(command) involving a single object.

As the single object rule (which allows only one number in { }) is broken, the system may be pre-programmed to respond to such cases by asking 'Which one?', and outputting the cause of the quandry.

In summary, the parsing-directed understanding programs are designed mainly to keep track of the meaning of the input statements, and to respond in a predefined way to the results of the computation. However, the word 'understanding' should not be interpreted in too literal a fashion here. The human meaning of the word has overtones that relate language to experience; language-understanding systems only relate the input to a database and a carefully contrived set of responses. The illusion of understanding can be taken even further in the creation of expert systems – this is the subject of Chapter 6.

Summary

In some ways this chapter is central to the design of intelligent systems, as to date algorithmic models have been the sole vehicle for the implementation of computer schemes that are intelligent in some way. It has been seen that rapid searches of a widely branching nature (called 'tree searches') are at the heart of algorithms for game playing and problem solving, while artificial vision systems involve a good balance between algorithms that deal with low level images and those that hold structural meaning within the computer. Finally, language-understanding algorithms show the importance of programs that enable a user to interact with databases without the use of specialized machine programs.

It should be noted here that algorithms are not the only route for approaching intelligent systems. The potential for designing structures with emergent intelligent properties that are not algorithmic will be discussed in Chapter 7.

CHAPTER 5

Intelligent systems and automation

In this chapter the question 'What are intelligent systems for?' will be considered. This contrasts slightly with what has been dealt with so far, which has been somewhat theoretical in nature. Indeed, many of the ideas that make up the field of intelligent systems are theoretical. But this book is about the design of such systems. The design of any system is thought to imply that at some stage, someone is going to make such a system and that at some other point, someone is going to use it. The major application for a system that is intelligent is said to be the replacement of other intelligent, but living systems. This is a sinister thought, and it is the object of this chapter to examine the realities and dangers of such a replacement. There are generally three prevailing views on this subject: the coldly economic, the idealistic and the analytic.

The first of these views goes back to the coining of the word *automation* by a works manager of the Ford Motor Company. The object of replacing a human is to manufacture a particular object at lower cost. The argument centres on making the object available to more consumers, making them happy, while the company makes more money, making its shareholders happy. In the mid-sixties, Sir Leon Bagrit delivered a series of Reith Lectures for the British Broadcasting Corporation, amid growing fear of the spread of computers and the automation they implied. His was the second of the above views, presenting automation as an extension of man's abilities, leaving him employed and in control of the important parts of processes. The third view can be found amid the writings of Norbert Wiener, who coined the word and founded the philosophy of *cybernetics*. To Wiener this pursuit implied the study of men and machines from the same rigorous, mathematical standpoint. Many misquoted him as having drawn the comparison between man and machine and thus having laid down the basis for replacing man by machine. Nothing was further from his outlook. He refused to be drawn into the argument, maintaining that safeguarding men from menial tasks was a worthwhile result of automation. He was far too conscious of the fact that such an argument may be viewed differently by a manager and a workman. The latter may be happy with a menial task if the alternative is unemployment and penury. He argued that the best way is to develop as good an understanding of advancing techniques for automation as possible, so that choices can be made with a full knowledge of the consequences. This is the view which will be developed in this book.

The history of automation in some ways supports Bagrit's view that the successful introduction of machinery takes place where it extends man's otherwise limited abilities. This is evident from the discovery of the flint tool to the use of cotton-spinning machines during the 1760s. The insidious backlash of the Industrial Revolution came from the fact that the introduction of machinery placed power in the hands of those who could afford them. They, in turn, hired and fired manpower to optimize the work of the machines. Thus, rather than being an extension of the abilities of humankind, machines became an extension of the power of industrial leaders. Chaplin's film *Modern Times* is a wry comment on what this does to the freedom of less fortunate people, who almost became fodder for machines.

In the late 1950s it became clear that the digital computer offered real potential for extending productive effort beyond the capabilities of human intervention. This seemed to lie in two main areas: the control of machinery at speeds beyond the reaction times of men, and the rapid processing of information needed in the management of large plant containing many computer-controlled machines. This era saw the advent of numerically controlled machine tools, and the use of computers in process control, ie plant in which a physical substance flows and is treated as it goes along. An example of the latter on a large scale is the manufacture of soap flakes where droplets of a soapy liquid are dried as they drop down a wide production pipe. A computer may be employed to control factors such as pressure and temperature in as many as 500 points in the process.

The advent of the robot

The first industrial robot systems were in use by the late 1960s, and they are now accepted as standard manufacturing components in a large number of factories. These tend to be largely in the automobile industry, but not exclusively so. Curiously, however, most robots are devoid of much intelligence. They tend to operate on repetitive programs that are rarely changed, and are insensitive to changes in their workspace. Indeed, this is likely to be a major area of technological development over the next few years. Inexpensive processing power is likely to increase both the sensing power of robots, as well as their ability to cope with a high degree of variability in their tasks. Contrary to the predictions of the late 1960s, when it was thought that automation would be based on vast computers with tentacle-like connections to remote workplaces, the future is much more likely to lie with machines that have a great deal of local intelligence and, only as a secondary duty, communicate with each other through a communications network if and when necessary.

It is the robot that is likely to be the execution tool for such workplace intelligence. As such it merits closer scrutiny.

THE MANIPULATOR ARM

What is now known as a robot is typically a mechanical manipulator arm such as shown schematically in Figure 5.1. This is one of many possible arrangements for such arms. The six-axes arrangement is quite typical, although some simplified systems might have as few as two axes, and other specialized systems as many as twelve axes when awkward access space is unavoidable. Each axis is associated with a driving motor. These can be hydraulic, electrical or stepping motors, the latter being the most sophisticated. In fact, a stepping motor is the embodiment of a counter-type automaton. Stepping motors have a large number of stable positions, or states. Either a positive or negative pulse can be fed to the motor, one makes it go forward and the other backward by precisely one step. This is ideal for computer control, and the motors themselves, through their stable states, retain a memory of their position. Some stepping motor units incorporate a digital encoding disk, which, by an arrangement of photocells and light emitters shining through this encoder disk, can transmit back to the computer a precise binary encoded digit specifying the current position of the motor. This enables the programmer of the system to write instructions such as: 'Generate pulses for motor 3 until motor 3 position is . . .'

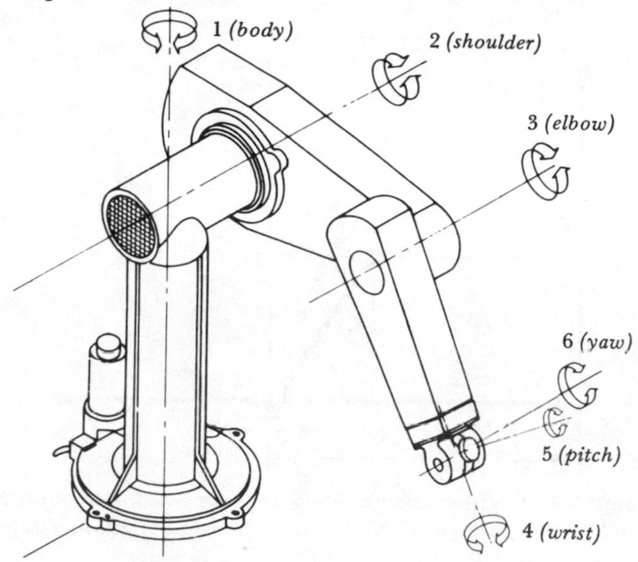

Figure 5.1. *A typical robot manipulator arm, the axes (or degrees of freedom) of the arm are identified*

The end point of the manipulator arm is called the *end effector,* and this can take many forms. Most often it is merely a simple or shaped gripper which acts as a pair of fingers. However, it could be a self-adjusting chuck, or a specialized tool such as a spray gun or a welding instrument.

POSITIONAL CONTROL OF THE MANIPULATOR ARM

The first task that needs to be resolved is for the computer to calculate the required positions for all the motors, when given a desired position and orientation of the end effector. In mathematical principle this is not difficult and involves the simultaneous solution of six equations. Techniques for doing this on computers take us a little too far afield. Nevertheless, it is possible to illustrate this by means of a simplified example. Figure 5.2. shows an arrangement having two degrees of freedom. The manipulator arm shown in Figure

5.1 has six such degrees of freedom, ie relative positions of adjacent limbs that can be independently controlled. Figure 5.2 illustrates that a degree of freedom does not necessarily imply a rotation. In fact, point P slides along the x-axis of some arbitrary system of coordinate axes, while limb PQ of length R rotates about P in the arbitrary x-y plane. The

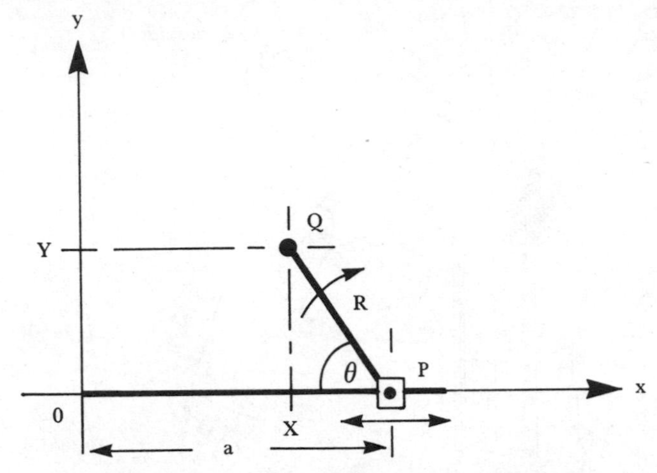

Figure 5.2. *A system having two degrees of freedom comprising a limb (PQ) which is able to move along a horizontal (0x)*

object for a processor is to calculate the values of *a* and θ, given a desired position for point Q. The equations that regulate these relationships are:

$$R \sin\theta = Y$$
$$a - R \cos\theta = X$$

These need to be solved in order to extract the desired values:

$$\theta = \sin^{-1} (X/R)$$
$$a = X + R \cos\theta$$

As long as the first of these equations is solved first, yielding the value of θ, the second may easily be solved. On a mathematical note, the solution to the first equation yields two values of θ, corresponding to the situation as shown in Figure 5.2 and the situation where $\theta' = 180° - \theta$. In this case $\cos\theta'$ becomes negative and $a = X - \cos\theta$. This is the alternative position with P being nearer to point 0 than to X.

Rather than have the computer solve these equations as

their solution is required, it is best to pre-calculate all possible solutions and simply look them up in a table. The look-up procedure normally requires very few instructions to a computer (technically, one 'fetch' cycle from store), while a calculation may require hundreds of times that number. However, there are penalties in terms of the amount of memory that is required for such a look-up operation. Assuming that a positional accuracy of 1/100 is available for the positioning of P (ie 100 'clicks' along its movement) and the angle θ is similarly controlled to an accuracy of 1 in 100 by a 100-state stepping motor, the total number of positions available to Q is 100 x 100, ie 10,000. As a first approximation this would require 10,000 words of store, each word needing to store a number between 0 and 100 for the value of θ and another similar number for the value of *a.* Each of these numbers requires seven bits, and if, say, one byte (eight bits) is allowed for convenience, it becomes clear that this task would be well within the capacity of a microprocessor (as in many home computers) which conventionally makes 64,000 bytes available. However, if six axes were to be controlled by means of a look-up table, a machine with 10^{12} words of 42 bits each would be required. This is out of reach of current computers. There are many clever ways of compromising between calculation and look-up. These somewhat specialized techniques are a little beyond the scope of this book and descriptions can be found elsewhere (Coiffet & Chirouze, 1983).

ROBOT APPLICATIONS

It is not appropriate for a book on intelligent system design to enter into a long discussion about robot applications. Nevertheless, it may be useful to take a brief look at the needs of production, so as to be better able to assess whether the use of intelligent systems would be advantageous (see also Engelberger, 1980).

In the case of metals, the main methods of producing goods of a given shape are by cutting and casting. Cutting is done using lathes on round objects, or milling machines for objects with flat surfaces. Traditionally, these tasks require skilled operators who are able to use these machines with great precision (aided by precision measuring instruments such as the micrometer screw).

A computer can control a tooling machine simply by energizing the actuators of the machine in a pre-defined sequence. Such systems are called *numerically controlled* tools. It is often the case that the required set of instructions is obtained automatically by monitoring the guidance of a machine by a skilled operator whilst he is doing the job manually. This enables the automatic system to reproduce the manufacture of an object in imitation of a skilled operator.

Much productive effort is concerned with the bringing together and subsequent assembly of components. This is where robots have proved to be a great success in the automobile industry, particularly for the welding of car bodies. However, they are less successful at assembly where precision fits need to be made. In order to overcome the lack of sensory power of most robots, parts that are to be assembled together in a closely fitting way need to be redesigned so as to carry guiding channels. Although this aids assembly it can severely detract from the cost benefits that could be generated by the use of robots.

Another major application for robots is the *pick and place* task. This generally assumes that parts are delivered (often by conveyor belt) to a precise location from which a robot manipulator can pick them up and place them in a predetermined position. Filling the tray of a chocolate box, from chocolates delivered in the right order to the pick-up point, is a good example of this. A task that is rather difficult for a blind manipulator arm is that of bin-picking. This involves picking parts out of bins in which many such parts lie in a disordered fashion.

A large amount of production effort is concerned with the inspection of manufactured goods: checking for correctness of an assembled object and checking for blemishes. Robots are currently used to carry out shape tests on assembled car bodies, by bringing a pressure-sensing probe into contact with the body under very carefully controlled position selection. It will be argued in the next section that improved sensing for robots, particularly visual sensing, is a major step in designing better, more intelligent machines. Certainly, inspection tasks such as mentioned here would benefit in an obvious way.

INTELLIGENCE FOR ROBOTS

Much use is being made of robots in industry on what might

be called *open loop.* This refers to the way in which manipulator arms can go about their preprogrammed routines with virtually no feedback from the environment in which they operate. Increased intelligence in such systems is fundamentally based on the provision of sensory feedback from the environment. Ultimately, this must include feedback not only from the object that is being manufactured, but also from a human supervisor who may wish to express himself in natural language. In technical terms such feedback provides *branching information* for what would otherwise be single-track programs. For example, an operator may wish to describe a task such as:

> '*Find* the casting for the outer part, insert it into the lathe, cut outer casing *until* diameter 0.5 cm has been achieved *then* polish *until* a reflectance of 90% is achieved, *then* unload and *find* inner casing for next process. ...'

The words 'until', 'then' and 'find' imply a change in the task (branching) that clearly requires sensory feedback from the environment.

Geometrical vision systems

In what follows, three generations of vision system will be defined, and some of these anticipate developments from predictions of feasible advances in the design of intelligent systems.

THE FIRST GENERATION

Several vision systems became commercially available in the early 1980s. These are preprogrammed to calculate the geometrical properties of crisp objects in their field of view, see for instance a, b and c in Figure 5.3. These systems assume that parameters such as the area, perimeter, number of holes, major radius, etc of all black objects in the (white) field of view are to be calculated. The parameters of the holes can also be calculated and the entire result output as a list of features.

It is clear that such a process would yield a list of features that varies greatly for a, b and c (see Figure 5.3). Such features can be stored and the orientation and position of the objects calculated for similar objects that occur in the field of view at a subsequent time. The implications are that very careful attention must be paid to lighting and cleanliness, in order not to distort the measurement procedure. Unfortunately, even under carefully controlled conditions the data derived from a television camera tends to look rather like that shown in Figure 5.3d. The system would have to equate this image with that shown in Figure 5.3c. Clearly, this cannot be done by the geometrical algorithm mentioned earlier, as this would report the presence of a large number of objects of irrelevant dimensions. In order to combat such deficiencies, geometrical vision systems are now endowed with sophisticated image-processing algorithms which remove small specks, close gaps, and trace the outlines of objects viewed by the camera. To appreciate the complexity of the task it is worth looking at some typical processing times that can be achieved with such systems.

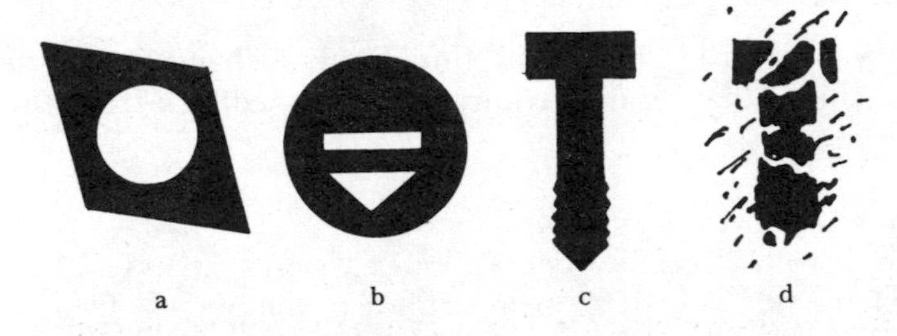

Figure 5.3. *Silhouettes of a number of objects (a – c) with the image (d) of object c, as obtained using a television camera*

It is common to use commercially available television cameras which (in the UK) operate at 625 lines and generate one complete frame in 1/25th of a second. As the resolution in a vertical direction cannot exceed 1 in 625, and there would be little point in exceeding this resolution in the horizontal direction, it has become standard to extract a matrix of 512 x 512 picture points (or *pixels*) from this image. The figure of 512 is used as it is the power of two nearest to, but less than, 625. Each picture point is then turned into an eight-bit digit (byte). Therefore, to store one frame of the image, it is necessary to have 256 kilobytes of memory. This immediately implies that microprocessors of the 16-bit-per-word type, or greater, are required.

Imagine the following simple operation. A window of two horizontally adjacent bytes is to be scanned over the stored image in order to look for edges in the image. The program would use two memory locations into which the bytes are transferred from store. These two are compared and if the difference is greater than a predetermined value, the presence of the position of the detected edge is stored. Without going into details, it may be estimated (optimistically) that about 20 machine cycles per pixel are needed. For some time to come it is unlikely that even the most sophisticated micro-processors of the type used in geometrical vision systems will exceed 8×10^6 machine cycles per second. It therefore turns out that the above operation is likely to take between 0.5 and 1.0 seconds. Since this operation may be only a fraction of the work that needs to be done in order to generate a complete list of geometrical features, it is hardly surprising that such schemes require several seconds to access an image. This tends to limit the applicability of the procedure as, on conveyor-belt systems, speeds of four to ten piece-part presentations per second (in pick and place operations) may be quite common.

It is therefore necessary to provide special-purpose (fast) hardware in situations where higher speeds are required. This makes production engineers wary of such devices, particularly if some of their other drawbacks are considered. The need for clean images and good lighting has already been mentioned. Geometrical properties will not easily distinguish between textures; this may be important in applications where one is dealing with leather or plastics, for instance. Special filtering techniques are required in the repertoire of image-processing software if branching on texture changes is required. A further difficulty is found with overlapping objects. The missing parts have to be regenerated by a process of template matching (for example) before their geometrical features can be estimated. This further adds to the computational overheads. It is evident therefore that it would be difficult to check for assembly completeness using a geometrical vision system — imagine detecting the missing part from a watch assembly, for instance. Such schemes are currently being researched in several laboratories, but require many man-years of programming by expert consultants. Even slight changes of task require a change to the complex computer software, making control over the use of vision equipment totally out of reach of the operator and the production engineer.

It seems then that first-generation systems, although quite useful in some special cases, are not 'intelligent' enough to form the basis of vision systems for robots in general.

ADDING ADAPTABILITY: THE SECOND GENERATION

The advancing generations of systems for robot vision do not represent a complete change of architecture between one generation and the next. It is more a case of building on the positive aspects of the previous generation and adding novel technology to overcome any drawbacks. Second-generation vision systems, which are likely to come into use in the mid-to-late 1980s consist of the geometrical program and frame-store arrangement of the first generation with the addition of adaptive *n*-tuple pattern recognizers as described in Chapter 4. The objective of such a combination is to remove the need for expert preprogramming when the task for the system is changed, allowing the operator and production engineer to do this by interaction with the system through a simplified keyboard (called a keypad). They are also able to show the system examples of what needs to be done through a TV camera.

To illustrate the operation of such a system consider the sequence of events that an operator may experience during the course of one task. Typical may be the sorting of the piece-parts of a kit into boxes. Say the parts are manufactured in batches of ten, each batch containing five parts that are to be loaded into a first box, and the other five into a second. It is convenient to turn out the parts one by one in arbitrary order into a grooved jig, where they lie in the field of view of the vision system and in a position from which they can be picked up by a robot gripper. The task for the robot is to pick the part out of the jig and place it in an appropriate box the right way up. Assuming that the parts can lie in the jig in only one of two positions it is clear that the robot is required to perform one of 20 possible operations, determined by the recognition of the part and its orientation. That is, the robot needs to recognize which of ten parts is present, and then decide whether it needs turning around or not. Clearly the technique does not require that the problem be constrained in this way (ie jigs, two orientations only, etc). This is merely convenient for the current explanation. It should also be noted that there is no need for the parts to be back-lit since the use of a second generation system is assumed, and that the decision of whether to turn the piece-part may be based on a parameter such as texture.

The first step is to issue a training schedule for the system. Either the operator or the production engineer can be responsible for this, and according to what has been suggested, there are 20 training steps required, one for each class of action. A little sophistication suggests itself at this point, as it would clearly be possible for the robot to train itself. To do this it would be given the ten parts in predefined locations and orientations. The manipulator could then be programmed by a single-branch program, to pick up the parts one by one and drop them in the jig in a known orientation. Part of this program is to enter training routines when the part is in the right position. The robot, continuing on its one-branch program would remove the part from the jig and replace it the other way round, repeating the training, and then go on to the next part, and so on.

An appropriate way to carry out this operation may be for the machine merely to store the training images and the actions required for them, so as to home in automatically on an optimal value of n, the crucial parameter of n-tuple recognition systems (see Chapter 4 for a discussion of this). Clearly, the training program would enable the vision machinery not only to set its own value of n (by looking for adequate performance on the training set), but also to decide whether fewer discriminators could be used. For example, in the pick and place operation described above, one discriminator could be used to decide whether the object needs to be turned, another whether the destination is the first or the second box, and then three further discriminators to determine the exact position within the selected box. This makes a total of five discriminators. The theoretical lower limit to this procedure is $\log_2 K$ discriminators for K classes.

One of the design criteria for such a system may be that the operator can be given a somewhat anthropomorphic understanding of what the machine is doing. For example, it may be appropriate that he should think that the machine 'can't think that fast' or that 'it is asking for more examples to make sense of these objects'. Much research is still required in the understanding and organization of this type of man-machine interaction.

ADDING INTELLIGENCE: THE THIRD GENERATION

The major limitation of the system described so far, has been the highly restricted channel of communication between the operator and the machine. It has been argued that requiring operators to communicate with vision systems via a computer language would be a burdensome imposition. However, the result of this has been that the operator has been delegated to communicate with the vision system through a simplified keypad and a television camera. Clearly, it would be highly desirable for the operator to be able to communicate with the machine in something approaching natural language. Indeed, this has been the subject of some work on artificial vision systems, as described in Chapter 4.

Although much of this work was developed in a context of somewhat ideal robotics (and as long ago as 1965) they have not found their way into industrial robot vision systems. There are several reasons for this. First, in order to create a database for the knowledge on which the linguistic interaction will be based, it is necessary to have a second-generation vision system. This, as shown in Chapter 4, turns objects in their raw, fuzzy state, as seen by a camera, into elements and symbols for the computer database.

A second major criticism is that the scenarios chosen for language understanding in the sphere of artificial intelligence are not close enough to that which might be required in a realistic, factory floor situation. To highlight the distinction between these two kinds of scenario, consider the following man-machine conversations. The first is of the type researched under the artificial intelligence banner, and the second may be closer to that which is required in reality.

Model 1: an artificial intelligence conversation

Operator: 'Pick up the green pyramid and put it in the white box'
Robot: 'OK'
Operator: 'Now put the lid on the box'
Robot: 'Which lid do you mean?'
Operator: 'The white lid'
Robot: 'OK'
(etc, etc)

Model 2: a third-generation vision system

1. Operator: 'This is a box of washers'
2. Robot: 'OK'
3. Operator: 'Are you capable of picking up the washers from the box, one at a time?'
4. Robot: 'Yes, with 80% confidence, therefore, if I notice that I have failed I can repeat the operation until it succeeds. By the third attempt my confidence should be 99.2%'
5. Operator (moving the box of washers to the top left corner of the field of vision): 'This is the position of the box for the next operation'
6. Robot: 'OK'
7. Operator (driving the conveyor belt forward until the top of an engine casing assembly appears in the lower half of the field of view): 'This is an engine casing'
8. Robot: 'OK'
9. Operator: 'When it gets to this position issue a halting signal for the conveyor belt mechanism'
10. Robot: 'OK, but if I do, the engine casing will have moved forward, please position it in this advanced position if further action is required'
11. Operator: 'This is the expected position, ± 3mm'
12. Robot: 'OK'
13. Operator: 'I shall point with this pointer (cursor, if necessary) to six positions where you must fit washers on the upright bolts that you see end-on'
14. Robot: 'OK'
15. Operator: 'Please confirm fitting positions' (moves casing slightly)
16. Robot: 'OK' (places cursor on screen in positions indicated)
17. Operator: 'Carry out one assembly run'
18. Robot: 'OK' (does it)
19. Operator: 'At the end of an assembly, take a close look at the washers. If they are different from the way they are now, sound an alarm'
20. Robot: 'OK'

The first striking difference is the generality with which this conversation can take place. Artificial intelligence has come up only with methods of conversation based on predefined series of shapes such as flat-sided objects. It is the power of second-generation vision systems that extends this range. Also, the nature of the linguistic transaction cannot rely solely on syntax-guided set operations (as described in Chapter 4). Here a kind of funnelling of the various ways of expressing a statement or command into one standard expression needs to be carried out. For example in line 3,

'Can you pick up ...' could have been an alternative way of saying 'Are you capable of picking ...' Such funnelling procedures need to be researched fully, but it might be predicted that with the falling costs of computer memory devices, it will be possible to create large look-up tables that standardize these alternative forms. Whatever the case, the sentence is translated into a database search triggered by the phrase 'picking up the washers' and a recognition of the image containing the washers. The target of the search is a record of a previous search of this kind and the success rate of the performance then achieved.

This is a general design principle for third-generation vision systems. They must never cease updating their databases, which makes the efficient storage of information a vital target for advancing technology. It is in lines such as line 7 that the knowledge database of the machine is developed, adding an understanding of the concept 'engine casing' to its store. Subsequent questions about the machine's ability to recognize engine casings would be positively answered.

In line 10 there is an indication that there is a need for the robot to anticipate the sequence of some events. It is important that this knowledge (data) is able to be input into the computer in more than one way. For example, either the operator could foresee that the overshoot might occur and simply prime the machine for it, or the need may arise from an inability of the machine to carry out a previous task. The rest of the conversation is effectively the programming of the machine to carry out a specific task. This incorporates the operator's awareness that the best that could be done if the operation has failed is to call him for further instruction.

It is important not to develop the impression that the activity described above is actually an example of an existing system. It still remains an aim for what has become known as fifth-generation computing: a phrase first used in Japan to describe targets for intelligent systems that make sense in the context of industrial production.

Now some general design principles will be described for a third-generation vision system, as part of a fifth-generation computing system (there are more generations of computers since they have been around longer than vision systems). [Chapters 6 and 7 will concentrate on the way in which storage of knowledge may be achieved in conventional computing systems (expert systems) and on novel methods and theories that should make the conversation between man and machine more plausible than it is at present.]

Architectures for automated systems

A *top-down* method of describing an ideal architecture for a computing system for intelligent automation, will be taken. This means that the initial description takes place at the most general and least detailed level. This is illustrated in Figure 5.4. The most general notion here is that the aim of the complete system is to receive data from a real but fuzzy world, in which items are generally in evidence as a result of the generation of some sensory data. A helpful aspect of such a world is that it contains people who, through the use of a keyboard, can help the system to identify its world. The system itself, on the other hand, has two distinct duties: to take action through, say, a robot manipulator arm, or to provide opinions for the benefit of the human components of the world. Clearly, the action could be directed towards other machinery such as numerically controlled tools or flexible manufacturing systems.

The intelligent machine itself is shown as consisting of two parts: the *image processing/pattern recognition system (IP/PR)* and the *intelligent knowledge-based system (IKBS)*. The former is what has been dubbed so far as a second-generation vision system, and the latter refers to intelligently organized databases (as will be discussed in Chapter 6). Although as discussed earlier IP/PR systems have a use on their own, it is unlikely that a realistic IKBS system can achieve a useful performance without the presence of an IP/PR at its front end. The main task for the IP/PR system is to package sensory information into either prototype images or simple symbolic descriptions of such images or their constituent parts. The word 'image' should be taken in a broad sense: it could refer to speech patterns obtained from a microphone, or tactile information from a pressure sensor.

A particularly important feature of such an architecture is that not only does the IP/PR system pass data on to the IKBS, but the latter can also control the former. A typical application of this arrangement is a two-step process where a broad class is recognized first, passed on to the IKBS, and this instructs the IP/PR to concentrate on a localized area of

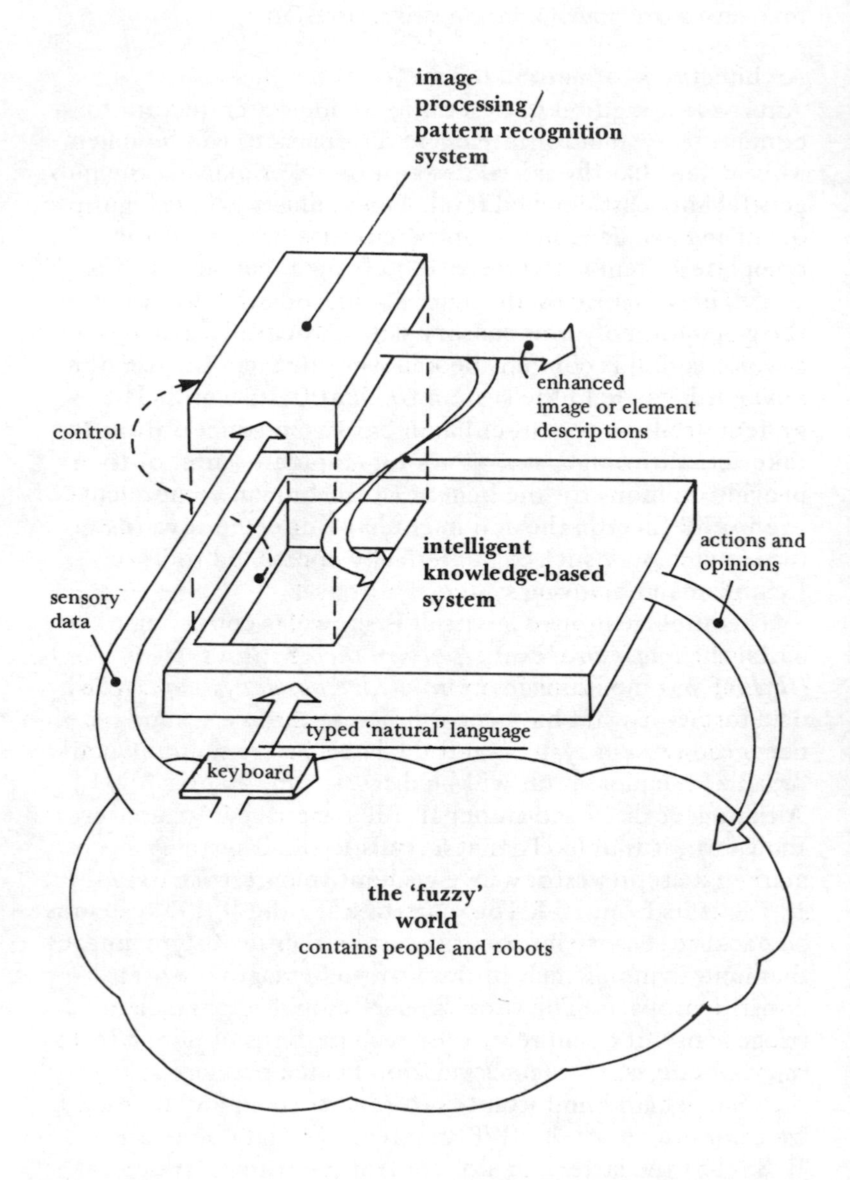

Figure 5.4. *An architecture for an intelligent automated system*

the image in order to refine the decision. As an example, in a printed-letter recognition task, the first response of the IP/PR system may be 'the O or Q class'. The IKBS may then apply controls to the IP/PR to drive a window into the lower part of the image to detect the presence or absence of the 'tail' and consequently confirm whether the letter is a Q or an O. Similarly, if both the identity of a face and its expression are to be detected, this can be done by appropriate window control from IKBS to IP/PR: switching a window to the area of the mouth to identify a smile once the face has been recognized.

Delving deeper into the system, the central point of interest is the way in which the IP/PR system is capable of generating enhanced images or image prototypes. An image enhancement task has already been described in the section on first-generation vision systems: the edge-seeking task. To reiterate, this would be a slow process for a high-resolution image. It is therefore envisaged that the image processing side of the IP/PR system would be a system of regularly connected processor cells such as shown in Figure 5.5a.

Such systems are currently being developed under names such as the Distributed Array Processor (DAP) and the Cellular Logic Image Processor (CLIP). The latter performs some of its operations in an *asynchronous* mode, ie it relies on a fast propagation of information in the array for data that need to propagate, and it does this in between the main 'beats of the clock' of the system.

Some details of the architecture of the IP/PR scheme are shown in Figure 5.6. The CLIP system would fit into the box marked fast processor, while an adaptive pattern recognition system such as WISARD (see Chapter 4) would reside in the box marked adaptive image processor. A set of frame-stores that hold digitized images obtained from the input transducers (cameras and microphones, etc) provide temporary image memories for the system to work on. This is particularly important in the generation of prototype images or sketches as required by the IKBS (for linguistic processing, for example).

It is the task of the adaptive image recognizer to generate prototypes. A simplified explanation of this process follows, although there are many reports on the subject for those interested in the finer detail (see Boden, 1977; Aleksander,

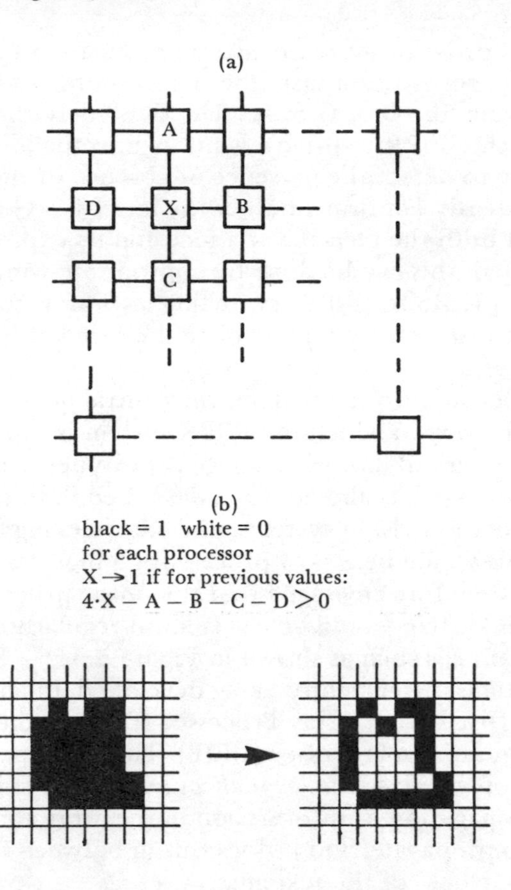

Figure 5.5. *(a) A parallel cellular processor; and (b) an edge detection operation*

1983; Duff, 1983). It was shown in Chapter 4 that *n*-tuple adaptive systems are taught code words that become associated with incoming patterns. By increasing the code word to the size of an image, this associative property can be used to relate prototypes or sketches to fuzzy input images. The image learning line of Figure 5.6 ensures this, while the image lines connecting the adaptive image recognizer to the frame-stores transmit its attempts at generating the prototypes of pattern variants seen at the input of the system. For example, the system may be taught to issue a sketch of a fork for several forks in the field of view on which the system is trained, one fork after another. A similar treatment may be carried out for spoons. Subsequently, on seeing a previously unseen spoon, the system is likely to respond with as much of the spoon prototype as it can. This procedure is illustrated in Figure 5.7. A useful property of this type of architecture is the feedback loop from the image output of the adaptive image recognizer back through its input via the frame-stores. Put simply, this is capable of recognizing imperfections in the self-generated prototype and correcting the defects in subsequent cycles of the system (this is also illustrated in Figure 5.7).

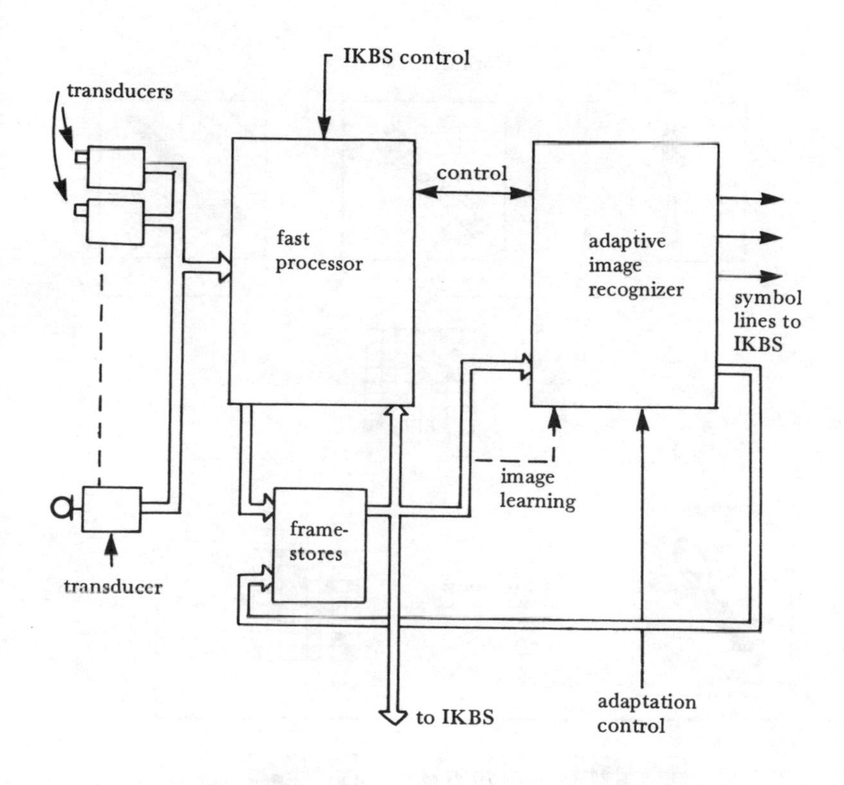

Figure 5.6. *Some details of the IP/PR architecture; =, image lines; –, control lines*

It is the adaptation control line that determines whether the

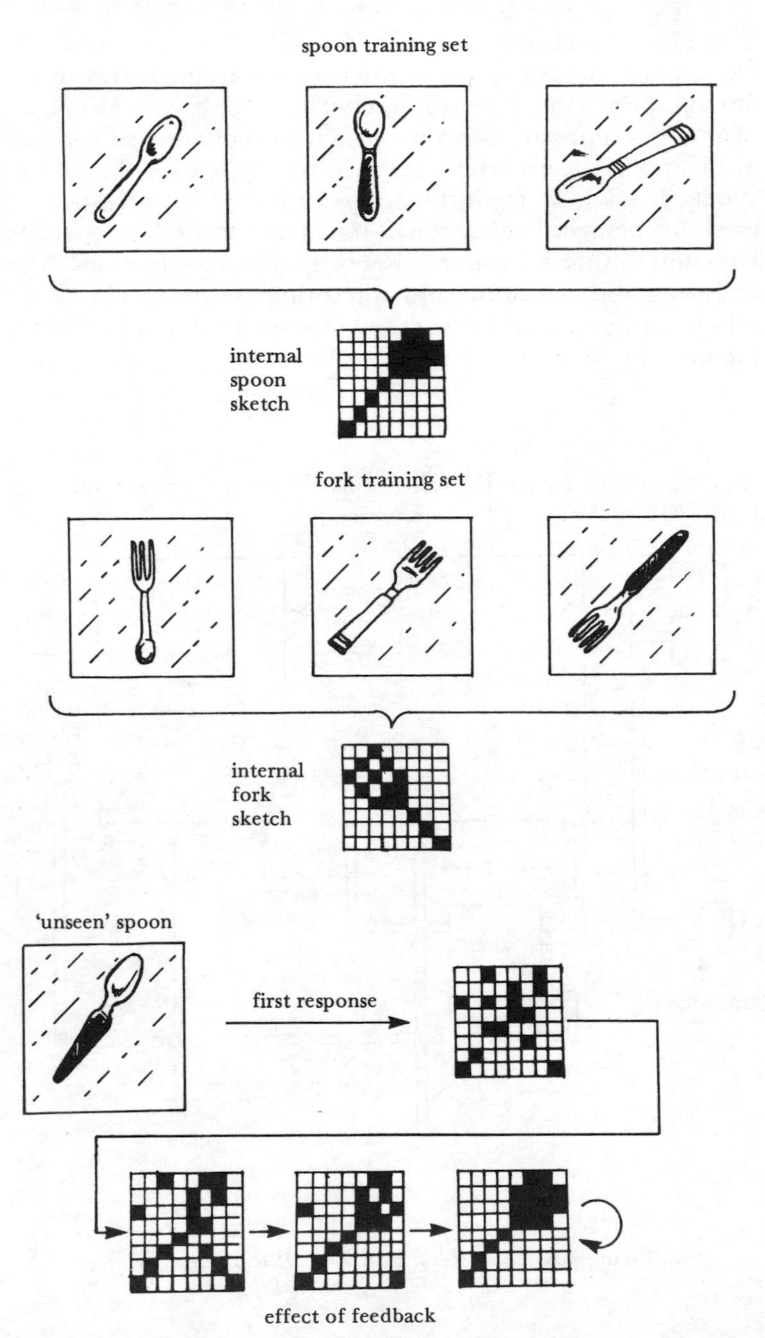

Figure 5.7. *The use of internal sketches for object recognition*

system is in a decision-learning or an image-learning mode. In the case of the former it is the decision that is transmitted through symbol lines to the IKBS, while in the case of the latter, it is the final image in one of the frame-stores.

Summary

Much of the drive for the development of intelligent systems has stemmed from the possibility of aiding the manufacture of goods. In this chapter we have considered the sort of intervention that computer-based systems might make. The robot manipulator arm has been seen as a mechanical device that is ideally structured as a general purpose replacement for the human arm. Indeed, the provision of processing power to aid this muscle has been the central concern here. Ways of dealing with sensory (mainly vision-based) information have been described in terms of currently available systems, those near commercial exploitation, and targets for the future. The architectures that are needed to achieve the desired processing in real time have been described and have been shown to consist of three major elements: image processing, pattern recognition and intelligent knowledge-based systems. The last of these subjects will be expanded on in Chapter 6. Here we end with a summary of the way in which these three functions may be involved in various tasks (not all of which are industrial!).

application	*PR task*	*IP task*	*IKBS task*
security* voice face signature intruder	recognition (100%)	–	–
medical cytology texture clean piece parts	–	image transformations (100%)	–
medical body shape monitoring (eg during pregnancy)	measurement (80%)	correction and enhancement (20%)	–
industrial pick and place	recognition (60%)	position correction (40%)	–

application	*PR task*	*IP task*	*IKBS task*
assembly by robot	arm control (50%)	window drive and enhancement (50%)**	—
assembly quality control	measurement (50%)	window drive (50%)	—
creation of sketch-like databases	window content classification and normalization (40%)	window drive and texture analysis (30%)	collation of results (30%)
conversational robot control	voice recognition, symbol generation (50%)	window drive and some analysis (10%)	language understanding (40%)
information technology: telephone, voice control, visual conference, etc	reading and recognition (50%)	—	model reference (50%)***

* The security applications refer to verification against identification cards or against reference images (eg in airfields where intruders are to be detected).

** This refers to the use of high-resolution fields in low-resolution fields whose positioning needs to be controlled.

*** This implies some programmer-constructed models.

CHAPTER 6

Models of expertise

In recent years, the focal point of artificial intelligence has been the realization that an intelligent response by *human* standards implies the storage in computers of *human* knowledge. This has led to research into efficient ways of storing and interacting with such data. This activity has also sharpened some of the aims of artificial intelligence through the notion that computer-captured knowledge is a marketable commodity. If the knowledge of an expert can be encapsulated in a program, and the program stored on a simple (floppy) magnetic disk, then this knowledge can be made available to non-experts.

This has two immediate attractions: it provides a guiding facility and an educational aid for the non-expert. Such systems are called *expert systems* and form the basis of much current research in artificial intelligence. It may be argued that such a program provides little over and above the facility offered by a good manual or a textbook. The overriding attraction, of course, is the fact that a computer-stored expert system is automatic. Where with a manual or a textbook the user must digest the information and find his own way around it, an expert system guides the user right into the centre of the required information via a route determined by a question-and-answer sequence. As an example, take the following 'item' of knowledge as it might appear in an automobile trouble-shooting manual (somewhat simplified here).

> A petrol engine, given that the fault is in the ignition circuit, will not start but will turn over. The causes of the fault may be:
> 1 there is a break in the low-tension cables,
> 2 there is a break in the high-tension cables,
> 3 the condenser has shorted.
>
> If a bulb placed across the distributor points lights when the points are open, the fault is not 1 or 2. K1

A reader of the manual would try to understand its contents and develop his own strategy for dealing with the fault. On the other hand, were he equipped with a computer that contained knowledge K1 in its database, a conversation would be possible, as follows:

Machine:	'State the symptoms'
User:	'The engine turns over but does not start'
Machine:	'Test the points voltage with a bulb in the usual way'

At this point the user may get inquisitive about the machine's line of reasoning and ask a question:

User:	'Why?'
Machine:	'For the time being, I am assuming that the fault is in the ignition circuit, in which a break in the low-tension circuit or a short-circuit capacitor may be the cause. The bulb test, if positive, will rule out this possibility'

This points to a major desirable characteristic of expert systems. They must be capable of explaining why they are providing a certain piece of advice. We shall see later that this is organized through a technique of back-tracking through the store of knowledge. The main aim here is to indicate how such storage systems may be organized to represent human knowledge, and how such knowledge may be entered and later retrieved in a controlled fashion. It should not be thought that it is the linguistic propriety of the above conversation that is difficult or, indeed, at stake in such work. It is the programming of logical statements and causal sequences that needs to be modelled and programmed. Without it, the system would operate at the non-expert level of ELIZA as described in Chapter 1.

It would be desirable if, while the knowledge of the system is being built up within it, this could be done in natural or near-natural language. However, as seen in Chapter 4, this is still an unresolved problem if the domain of discourse is not strongly curtailed. Therefore, the first question that arises is whether conventional computer languages are adequate for knowledge-based communication with an expert system.

Most computer languages provide facilities for creating arrays. It is through this that knowledge databases could be built up. This requires a great deal of computing 'overhead' in terms of needing to declare the size of arrays, their type and so on. This would mean that the programmer would spend more time in structuring his program to represent the knowledge, rather than building up the knowledge base. It is for this reason that special languages have been developed whose syntax is particularly suited to the expression of logical statements. The first of these, predicate calculus, comes straight out of a branch of mathematics that is used for ascertaining the validity of proofs and logic in general.

Predicate calculus

This is a rigorous mathematical language which involves both syntax and semantics about logical facts and their consequences. As seen in Chapter 3, when a language is defined it is important to specify its symbols and the structures involving them. In predicate calculus a 'sentence' is called a 'well-formed formula' or wff for short. These are made up of simpler 'atomic formulae' which, in turn, consist of *predicate symbols, variable symbols, function symbols* and *constant symbols.* Use is also made of brackets and commas, as will be shown, while the major operator symbols are called *connectives* as they serve to connect atomic formulae. Typically, such connectives are 'V' which reads 'or' and 'Λ' which reads 'and', the connective '⇒' is used for 'implies' and '—' for 'not'.

Staying in the field of automobile maintenance, it is possible to illustrate these concepts. For example, the phrase 'The battery energizes the starter motor' can be written as an atomic formula:

ENERGIZES(BATTERY,STARTERMOTOR).

Here, ENERGIZES is the predicate symbol that determines a relationship between the first constant symbol BATTERY and the second STARTERMOTOR, in that order. Variable symbols may be used when it is necessary to state generalities such as:

ENERGIZES(x,y)

where x and y are the variable symbols. This defines an entire class of relationships where the values of x and y could be BATTERY and STARTERMOTOR as earlier, but they could also be GENERATOR and ELECTRICSYSTEM or COIL-PRIMARY and COILSECONDARY.

Function symbols are used to express objects through their relationship to other objects. For example, 'Fuel for a petrol engine' may be expressed by the function symbol:

fuel(PETROLENGINE)

This allows the following (rather obvious) atomic formulae to be stated:

IS (PETROL, *fuel*(PETROLENGINE))
IS (DIESEL, *fuel*(DIESELENGINE))

To relate wff's or atomic formulae to the real world, they are said to have a value: *true* if the relationship holds and *false* if it does not. For example, ENERGIZES(BATTERY,HORN) evaluates as true while ENERGIZES(BATTERY,TYRES) is false.

Connectives are used to group atomic formulae together to form wff's. For example, one of the symptoms that may be relevant to K1 seen earlier, may be written as:

TURNSOVER(ENGINE)Λ – STARTS(ENGINE)

This reads 'The engine turns over and does not start.' It is also seen here that an atomic formula such as TURNSOVER (ENGINE) can have a single constant symbol. As a further example of the representation of K1, the notion 'It is either fault 1 or fault 3', the connective 'V' (or) is used:

IS(FAULT,1) V IS(FAULT,2).

The implication sign '⇒' is used to relate causes and effects. Thus, 'If the fault is (1) or (2) then a bulb test fails' may be expressed as:

IS(FAULT,1) V IS(FAULT,2) ⇒ FAILS(BULBTEST)

It is now possible to state the whole of K1 in predicate calculus form:

–START(ENGINE) Λ TURNSOVER(ENGINE)
Λ IS(ENGINE,PETROLENGINE) ⇒ FAULTY(IGNITION-CIRCUIT)
FAULTY(IGNITIONCIRCUIT) ⇒ IS(FAULT,1) V IS(FAULT, 2)
V IS(FAULT,3)

where 1 = LTBREAK
2 = HTBREAK
3 = CONDENSERSHORT

also $\neg$PASSES(BULBTEST) $\wedge$ PASSES(CONDENSERTEST)
$\Rightarrow$ IS(FAULT,1)
PASSES(BULBTEST) $\wedge$ PASSES(CONDENSERTEST)
$\Rightarrow$ IS(FAULT,2)
PASSES(BULBTEST) $\wedge$ – PASSES (CONDENSERTEST)
$\Rightarrow$ IS(FAULT,3)

All that has been done so far has been the representation of the knowledge in a standard form which enables the machine to store the symbols and the relationships between them. This may be seen as the phase during which the knowledge is programmed into the system. To retrieve and use this knowledge, some further standardization is required. There are several ways of achieving this. In the next section a method is described that utilizes *production rules* similar to those used in the linguistic structures of Chapter 3.

Production rules

A production rule system requires a standard way of representing the logical database. It restricts the left-hand side of the production to wff's known as *clauses.* These contain only atomic formulae connected by $\wedge$ connectives. The right-hand side can be an *action,* a *conclusion* or a *suggestion.* Actions are given as the end points of a reasoning process. In automobile maintenance an action may be the statement 'The engine needs replacing'. A conclusion, on the other hand, is an intermediate step in a knowledge-based interaction. For example, 'The fault is likely to be in the ignition circuit' is such a statement. A suggestion is an indication that if more information is supplied, the program can proceed with its investigation. For example, 'Carry out a battery test and enter the result', is, indeed, a suggestion.

Returning to the clausal structure of these production rules, it should be noted that this is not too restrictive a requirement. Logical statements can generally be transformed into clause form. Take the wff:

$$A \wedge (B \vee C) \Rightarrow P \wedge Q$$

where A, B, C, P and Q are atomic formulae. To transform the right-hand side, the rule from symbolic logic can be used:

$$X \Rightarrow P \wedge Q \text{ becomes } X \Rightarrow P \text{ and } X \Rightarrow Q$$

Substituting for X:

$$A \wedge (B \vee C) \Rightarrow P$$
$$A \wedge (B \vee C) \Rightarrow Q$$

The left-hand side may be rewritten as:

$$(A \wedge B) \vee (A \wedge C)$$

as a direct result of the distributive law in symbolic logic. Appealing again to symbolic logic, the theorem $X \vee Y = P$ may be written as two wff's, $X \Rightarrow P$, $Y \Rightarrow P$, providing a complete breakdown of the wff into its clausal form:

$$(A \wedge B) \Rightarrow P$$
$$(A \wedge C) \Rightarrow P$$
$$(A \wedge B) \Rightarrow Q$$
$$(A \wedge C) \Rightarrow Q$$

This procedure may now be applied to the item of knowledge K1. For clarity the following abbreviation is first applied to the atomic formulae:

START(ENGINE)	:	SE
TURNOVER(ENGINE)	:	TE
IS(ENGINE,PETROLENGINE)	:	EP
FAULTY(IGNITIONCIRCUIT)	:	FI
IS(FAULT,1)	:	LT
IS(FAULT,2)	:	CD
PASSES(BULBTEST)	:	BT
PASSES(CONDENSERTEST)	:	PC

The clausal form of K1 can be transformed into this form. There are four conclusion clauses and two suggestion clauses:

1. (conclusion) $(-SE \wedge TE \wedge EP) \Rightarrow FI$
2. (conclusion) $(-BT \wedge CT) \Rightarrow LT$
3. (conclusion) $(BT \wedge CT) \Rightarrow HT$
4. (conclusion) $(BT \wedge -CT) \Rightarrow CD$
5. (suggestion) $FI \Rightarrow BT$
6. (suggestion) $FI \Rightarrow CT$

The suggestion clauses are new in the sense that they do not explicitly appear in the predicate calculus formulation of K1. These are needed to link the conclusion in line 1 with the conclusions in lines 2,3 and 4. It now becomes possible to follow the operation of the program through these production rules. As before, the input is a statement that the petrol engine turns over but does not start. The process of translating this into symbols SE, TE, etc is left undefined for the moment. It must result in (–SE Λ TE Λ EP). The program proceeds to look for a match on the left-hand side of the stored rules. It finds it in rule 1 and changes its current state to FI. As this is not a suggestion but an intermediate conclusion, the program searches for a match for its new state. It finds two and this can make it output: 'Do the bulb test' and 'Do the condenser test'. It is at this point that the user may need a little hand-holding, to build up confidence in the program. So he might ask 'Why'. This is a signal for the machine to search backwards from the last conclusion and output the answer, 'Because both these tests are for a faulty ignition circuit' (end of first back-tracking step); 'Ignition faults are likely when petrol engines turn over but do not start' (rule 1 has been found again).

When the machine has returned to rules 5 and 6, an inquisitive user may ask 'What can I expect'. This is a clue to the program to anticipate the outcome of the suggested tests. One way in which it can do this is to seek out all the rules that contain the current suggestions and spell them out. This would lead to computer output of the kind: 'A failed bulb test and a passed condenser test imply a fault in the low-tension circuit'; 'A passed bulb test and ...'; etc.

In summary, it is now possible to see how programs may be constructed that approach the sort of linguistic interaction that was illustrated at the beginning of the chapter. The only part of the explanation that has not been fully explained is the way in which a program translates from near-natural language into a symbolic formulae it can handle, and vice versa. This is a matter of storing standard responses, or responses obtained during an input session. A rather complex interaction during input might be as follows:

Machine:	'What is the next conclusion for which you wish to provide a precondition?'
User:	'A faulty ignition circuit' (A)
Machine:	'Provide a single word predicate and constant for this condition'
User:	'FAULTY(IGNITIONCIRCUIT)' (B)

At this point the machine must store A and B related to one another in a *translation* database. It may also find its own abbreviated symbol (say, FI) for B. It is this relationship that is used in outputs such as '... these tests are for *a faulty ignition circuit ...*'

PROLOG

So far, expert systems have been described as having an external near-language interface, and an internal operation based on logical statements which obeys the laws of logic. In 1975 researchers based at the University of Marseilles published a report on a language called PROLOG. Developed by a computer science team at the university, this language enables predicate formulae in their clausal form to be input directly. This language is being used increasingly for writing expert systems.

A typical program in PROLOG may be thought of as a list of clauses which could be atomic formulae or clausal rules. For example, consider once again the subject of automobile maintenance, the following could be lines of program in PROLOG (this is an illustration only, and the mechanically minded reader should not worry too much about the sense it might make to a motor mechanic).

```
Energizes(x,y) := Connected (x,y)
Energizes(x,z) := Connected (x,y), Energizes (y,z)
Connected(battery,horn)
Connected(battery,generator)
Connected(generator,coilprimary)
Connected(generator,lights)
```

The first two lines are what programmers call *procedures* – they carry out an operation on variables that have to be specified somewhere else. What the first line says is, 'It is true that x energizes y, if it is true that x is connected to y.' The last four lines are data which are stated to be true. The program itself is set off by the provision of a query such as: Energizes(battery,?). This is the programmer's way of asking the system to list all those objects that are energized by the *battery*. As a first step the program takes note of all the rules that match with the predicate part of the query (ie energizes). It then proceeds to work with the first rule as far as it can by transforming *Energizes(battery,?)* into *Connected(battery,?)*. A scan down the data generates matches for '?' evaluating to *horn* and *generator*. These are output as part of the answer. The program then graduates on to the second rule and transforms Energizes(battery,?) into:

Connected(battery,y), Energizes(y,?)

It then tries to fit in all true values of the intermediary symbol y. For example, an attempt at letting y be *horn* fails as no value of '?' satisfies the atomic formula:

Connected(horn,?).

However, if y now assumes its alternative value, *generator,* both *coilprimary* and *lights* evaluate as being valid. These are then added to the output list.

PROLOG is not limited to logical operations only, it can carry out most of the tasks that may be required of any high-level programming language. The only difference is that the predicate format for all expressions may be retained. For example, where in some other language one might write (A + B), in PROLOG this may be written both as (A + B) and +(A,B).

A further attraction of PROLOG to practitioners of artificial intelligence is the way in which tree structures (as found in problem solving and game playing, see Chapter 4) may be represented. This makes use of brackets in the clause-like structure, as will be seen. To illustrate this point, take the following set of grammatical rules:

s	:=	np vp	where:
np	:=	a n	s stands for (sentence)
vp	:=	v np	np stands for (nounphrase)
a	:=	'a'/'the'	vp stands for (verb phrase)
n	:=	'engine'/'body'/'piston'	a stands for (article)
v	:=	'needs'	n stands for (noun)
			v stands for (verb)
			'symbol' is a terminal symbol

This is the grammatical structure that generates sentences such as 'The engine needs a piston.' In PROLOG, this entire sentence structure may be expressed as:

s(np(a(the),n(engine)),vp(v(needs),np(a(a),n(piston))))

Clearly, this is a most sketchy statement of the nature of PROLOG. It has been included only so that the link between the mathematical language of predicate calculus and a real programming language is made (for more details see Clark & McCabe, 1983).

The use of probabilities

Human knowledge is not always definite and definable in strictly logical terms. Even when the weather forecast is 'Tomorrow will be cloudy with showers' this means that out of all the weather events that could happen tomorrow, 'cloudy with showers' is the most likely. Two points arise. First, how can likelihoods and probabilities be built into a logical database? And second, it is necessary to have methods that can calculate probabilities from observed data, or data provided by several experts all of whom may not immediately agree.

Some aspects of the first question may easily be accommodated within the ways of writing logical programs that have been covered earlier. It is quite possible to express:

predicate(x) ⇒ conclusion(y)

where y is, say,

'probability p of some cause c'.

For example, the following is admissible as a pair of logic statements:

–START(ENGINE) ⇒ FAULTY(ELECTRICS, 70%)
–START(ENGINE))⇒ FAULTY(CARBURATION, 30%)

On finding a –START(ENGINE) match the machine might output: 'There is a 70% chance that the fault is in the electrics and a 30% chance that it is in the carburation.'

There is a more subtle way in which an expert program can use probabilistic information by controlling the order in which suggestions are made. Consider once again the situation described earlier where, having concluded that a fault is in the ignition circuit (FI), the program found two left-hand matches: FI ⇒ CT and FI ⇒ BT. This causes the program to output both suggestions. Were the rules written probabilistically as:

FI ⇒ CT,70%
FI ⇒ BT,30%

the program would suggest that the condenser test be done first as this is likely to have a positive result and would so avoid further testing.

Returning to the weather forecasting problem, it is clearly

possible for a computer to be given a great deal of cause-and-effect data from which it extracts its own probabilistic information. For example, the following observations may be fed to an expert system for weather forecasting.

pressure (mbars)	*precipitation*	*pressure (mbars)*	*precipitation*
990	yes	1010	no
1000	no	1020	no
1000	yes	1030	no
990	yes	1010	no
1010	yes	990	yes

The way in which the statistical data is extracted depends on what the programmer decides. For example, he may wish to distinguish between high pressure (1010-1030 mbars) and low pressure (the rest). Then, because there is no precipitation for four out of the five cases in the high pressure range, the rule created from the data would be:

HIGH(PRESSURE) ⇒ NOPRECIPITATION, 80%

The difficulty with what has just been proposed is the lack of subtlety of the division of pressure into the 'high' and the 'low' set. The expert is forced to make a divisory decision in an area where he may wish to be more subtle. This brings to the fore a body of theory that was triggered off by precisely this need: the theory of *fuzzy sets.* This simple idea was first proposed by Lotfi Zadeh (1979) at Stanford University in the early 1960s, and elaborated in the UK by Ebrahim Mamdani (1974). In contrast to conventional set theory where the function 'belongs to' assigns objects to sets, in fuzzy set theory a 'degree of belonging' may be specified when making this assignment. For example, were one to define two sets 'tall people' and 'short people', given a person six feet tall one would assign him wholly (that is, using a multiplier of one) to the tall class. However, were he five feet nine inches tall the notion 'quite tall' may be expressed by applying a *belonging multiplier* of 0.8 for the tall class and 0.2 for the short class.

This multiplier notion should not be confused with the idea of a probability. There is no probability involved in saying that someone is quite tall. His height is known, it is in its description as a linguistic statement that the belonging multiplier is required. Applying this to the weather forecasting expert system, the scheme allows the user to specify the pressures by these multipliers as follows:

pressure (mbars)	*low multiplier*	*high multiplier*
990	0.9	0.1
1000	0.7	0.3
1010	0.5	0.5
1020	0.3	0.7
1030	0.1	0.9

These multipliers are used to evaluate X in:

HIGH(PRESSURE) = NOPRECIPITATION, X

as follows:

pressure (mbars)	*no/total*	*after multiplier*
1030	1/1	.9x1/.9x1
1020	1/1	.7x1/.7x1
1010	2/3	.5x.67/.5x1
1000	1/2	.3x.5/.3x1
990	0/3	.1x0/.1x1
		1.885/2.5 . . . totals

Hence, X=1.885/2.5 = 0.754. It is not implied that this result is any more accurate than the value of 0.8 obtained purely from the probabilities that resulted in a rough division between the low and high pressure sets. It is merely implied that this value more faithfully represents the expert's intention, having given him added flexibility in being able to specify more precisely 'high' and 'low'. Also, it is easy to appreciate that whereas the previously calculated value of 80% was truly a probability calculated from occurrence frequency of events, the value of X is a confidence factor which modifies the probability to fit in with a flexible definition of the event sets.

Finally, in this consideration of the use of probabilities as a way of capturing expertise, one finds an application for the probabilistic automata first encountered in Chapter 2. Again it may be helpful to illustrate the entire process starting with the interaction between the machine and the expert who is intending to input his knowledge.

Machine: 'Define the current state of affairs giving a reference label'
Expert: 'The engine will not start: NS'
Machine: 'State courses of action, giving labels'

Expert:	'Ventilate (v)* or choke (c)'
Machine:	'Name likely outcomes and probabilities, giving labels'
Expert:	'For (v) 30% leads to Start (S) and 70% back to No Start (NS) For (c) 60% leads to Start (S) and 40% leads to Flooding (F)'
Machine:	'Name courses of action and outcomes from (F)'
Expert:	'From (F),(c) returns to (F), 100% and (v) goes to (S), 100%'
Machine:	'Is (S) a desired state?'
Expert:	'Yes'
Machine:	'I now have full knowledge of how to get from (NS) to (S)'

Indeed, this knowledge may be represented as a probabilistic automaton as shown in Figure 6.1. From this stored knowledge, the system can work out that the safest way to start the car is to use the choke, and if the engine does not fire immediately, to ventilate it. The example would be even more realistic if a transition were included from NS to FB: flat battery! The reader might care to design such an automaton from an extended expert/machine conversation.

Known expert systems

The field of expert systems currently represents the major application of artificial intelligence. Here the most successful of these systems are briefly reviewed. But first, it is necessary to explain some of the terminology that exists in the evaluation of expert systems and to relate this to what has been said up to now.

In literature describing expert systems the term *generate and test* is often mentioned as the major way of searching knowledge databases. This refers to the way in which the current state of a quest for a target in the search tree may be represented as a state, and subsequent states are then generated by a blind application of fitting rules (this was discussed in the section on problem solving in Chapter 4). This makes up the *generate* part of the scheme. The *test* part is a tree-pruning process where constraints are applied to the newly generated states and a number may be removed, thus saving further searches. This is a half-way house between

* Ventilation is the process of depressing the accelerator so as to clear a cylinder chamber.

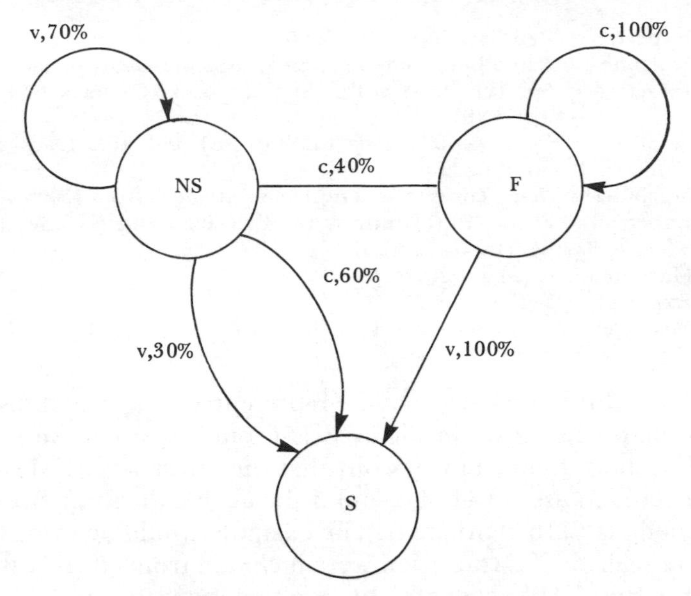

Figure 6.1. *A probabilistic automaton that describes acquired knowledge on how to start a car engine (NS, engine does not start; c, choke; F, engine flooded; V, ventilate cylinder; S, engine started)*

applying a proper evaluation criterion at each stage (as described in the section on game playing in Chapter 4) and an exhaustive rule-constrained search.

The constraints in the search are largely derived from *domain specific knowledge* which is the terminology used for the rules and facts that have been gathered during the building up of the database. This should be differentiated from the *inference engine,* which is the structure contained in the program for implementing the rules of logic in one of the several possible ways discussed earlier in this chapter.

The rules themselves are often referred to as being of the *situation* ⇒ *action* kind, which is a general way of describing most of the rule representations that have been used so far. Expert system designers sometimes refer to *grain size.* This refers to the complexity of the item of knowledge in a rule. For example, a rule such as:

NOSTART ⇒ ENGINEFAULT

is so small as to be meaningless to the domain specialist,

while:

NOSTART and SMOKE and NEWPLUGS and OLDPOINTS
⇒ DECOKE or VALVEGRIND or PISTONRINGREPLACE

is so large as to be almost incomprehensible. The art of designing expert systems rests with decomposing knowledge into optimally sized grains so as to be meaningful and comprehensible. This optimality makes for flexibility in changes in the database that may occasionally be necessary.

Another measure of the excellence of an expert system is the *line of reasoning.* This simply refers to the clarity with which the system replies to requests for justification.

DENDRAL

This has recently been described as the grandfather of expert systems. First developed in 1965 at Stanford University, it was designed to help chemists identify compounds from the readings taken from spectrometers. Given the output data from both a mass spectrometer and a nuclear-magnetic resonance spectrometer, the system is required to list possible atom-bond structures. The original data was obtained from expert users, while constraints on the range of answers may be supplied by any user, from a knowledge of the conditions under which a particular compound was created and tested. Thus, *situations* are particular atomic configurations and *actions* are fragmentations of these configurations. Each plausible fragmentation is linked to the originating situation by a probability-labelled link. Generate-and-test is the search regime adopted in this scheme. The knowledge base of the system consists of items such as rules for spectrometer effects, and rules for possible configurations of atoms. The program is in everyday use by chemists at Stanford University.

META-DENDRAL

Developed in the mid-1970s this work is a sequel by the Stanford team of their work on DENDRAL. Where in DENDRAL the rules for feasible molecule fragmentations in a mass spectrometer are derived from human experts, META DENDRAL is a system that generates such rules with the guidance and advice of the human experts. Primarily, examples of the fragmentation of known compounds are fed to the system which then uses its inferential programs to try to devise general rules. Generate-and-test is the adopted regime, where the constraints in the test phase may be supplied by the user.

MYCIN

This was developed in the mid-1970s at the Stanford Medical School. The task carried out by the system is one of relating symptoms of blood infections and diseases in the meningitis group to diagnoses and treatment plans. The knowledge is built up through consultations with human experts in this field and stored in the IF ... THEN manner described earlier in this chapter. The forward search is done in a generate-and-test manner, while the line of reasoning is provided by a process of backward chaining of rules, which was also described earlier in this chapter.

MYCIN has a partner program called TEIRESIAS which concentrates on knowledge acquisition. The innovative feature of this system is to seek out diagnoses with which the human experts disagree. It then seeks modifications by running backwards and forwards along the inference structure, altering a minimal number of IF ... THEN statements, until agreement is achieved.

A further point of interest of the MYCIN system is that it is able to answer both 'How?' and 'Why?' questions. 'Why?' questions lead the system to backtrack in order to explain to the user why a particular question has been asked. The answer provided by the system actually describes the *backward* search through the tree. A 'How?' question, on the other hand, provides an answer that describes the latest forward search (the line of reasoning) which has led the program to its current state.

PROSPECTOR

This system was developed in the late 1970s at the Stanford Research Institute to aid geologists in the evaluation of the excellence of an exploration site in respect of the existence of various types of ore deposits. The stored knowledge consists of elaborate models of the characteristics pertaining to certain classes of ore deposits. The knowledge base was contributed by experts in the field, who worked in collaboration with a consultant who was aware of the way in which the system was best able to accept information.

PROSPECTOR makes subtle use of probabilistic concepts, called *plausible relations* in the system (in contrast to *logical relations* which are based on the laws of logic, and were described earlier in this chapter). The system has been subjected to tests where it was compared to human experts, not involved in the creation of the knowledge base, and showed a remarkable degree of agreement.

OTHER EXPERT SYSTEMS

The development of expert systems is booming. Following in the wake of successes such as PROSPECTOR, expert systems are appearing in most fields of endeavour. A few of these are listed here to give the reader a feel for the vigour of this activity.

In bioengineering, systems such as MOLGEN are being developed to provide advice on likely combinations of DNA molecules, while GENESIS aids with gene-splitting experiments. In chemistry, SECS has been developed which is a system for planning synthesis strategies for the combination of organic molecules.

Expert systems are common in the computer industry itself, where fault diagnosis schemes (DART), system configuration advice (XCON), analysis of errors (SPEAR) and marketing assistance (XSEL) are beginning to feature significantly in increasing the profitability of their users. The IBM company has sponsored several USA universities to design expert systems that assist in the development of software and debugging aids.

Engineering design is another natural target for computer-stored expertise. Systems such as EURISKO and KBVLSI are typical aids to the design of silicon chips. In service industries too, expert systems such as LDS for legal claim adjustment and TAXMAN for advice in corporate law, are beginning to make an impact. In medicine, the success of MYCIN has been followed by systems that provide advice in areas other than diseases of the blood. Examples are electrolyte disorders (ABEL), general internal medicine (CADUCEUS), a causal network for glaucoma (CASNET), cancer chemotherapy (ONCOCIN), lung disorders (PUFF) and respiratory therapy (VM).

Summary

Under the guise of expert systems, this chapter has served to examine methods of storing knowledge generated by humans for use by other humans. Because the activity is finding a major commercial market, it is often hailed as the justification and ultimate application of many years of endeavour in artificial intelligence. However, it is necessary to sound a word of caution. It has been shown in this chapter that concern in this area centres on the efficient interpretation, storage and retrieval of information about knowledge domains that *can* be expressed as simple logical or probabilistic rules. There are, however, probably many more areas where computer aids of an advice-giving kind would be useful, but where knowledge cannot be encompassed in this simple way. Typical might be advice givers in computer aided design, where a designer requires not only bare knowledge, but also advice that suits his own particular way of innovation.

This implies a much closer interchange between the human and the computer, and a much more subtle method of adaptation within the machine. The design of such programs is still a matter for speculation and research – Chapter 7 will be devoted to such speculations.

CHAPTER 7

Future prospects

In the preceding chapters the central concern has been with the theoretical principles that need to be understood for the design of intelligent systems. These are mathematical in nature and are unlikely to change in the future. In answer to the question 'What is an intelligent system?', the current paradigm centres on artificial intelligence and expert systems, as described in Chapters 5 and 6. As a first step in looking towards the future, the permanence of this paradigm needs to be examined. The aim here is to anticipate likely changes and alternatives to the current mode of thought.

Paradigms and revolutions

The word *paradigm* was first used by Thomas Kuhn in his influential essay *The Structure of Scientific Revolutions.* He defined it as 'universally recognized scientific achievements that, for a time, provide model problems and solutions to a community of practitioners. In other words, he stressed the nature of a consensus that practitioners reach almost out of necessity, so that they can work and understand each other as a community. Kuhn also saw paradigms to be akin to political regimes: they may be overthrown if sufficient momentum is created either by the discovery of new, contradicting facts, or by the persuasiveness of people with new ideas. Such changes are seen by Kuhn as scientific revolutions, whose turbulent effect on the scientific community is akin to a significant change of political regime.

In the paradigm of intelligent systems, as exemplified by artificial intelligence and expert systems, there is a likely scientific revolution on the way. The pressure for such an event comes from the diminishing credibility of the way in which words such as intelligence and understanding are used in the context of artificial systems. The question was first raised at the beginning of this book where intentionality was seen as being an attribute that distinguished between current man-made intelligent systems and natural ones. We recall that intentionality is a word used to describe the human attribute of object-relatedness: that very personal use and acquisition of knowledge about objects in the real world. We further recall the example of the word *bacon,* which to a human being affords the memory of an experience of eating bacon. It is unlikely that a machine would ever have such an experience.

However, the question of how much towards intentionality can the attributes of a machine go, remains a real one. The rest of this chapter is concerned with the gap between intentional systems and non-intentional machines, and the way in which attempts to bridge this gap are likely to be responsible for a real shift in the intelligent systems paradigm.

Intentional machines

The central difficulty in the design of a machine that might ultimately exhibit intentionality has been described – consider the example of the bacon above. The notion of a bacon-eating machine designed for the purpose of giving meaning to the notion of machine intentionality seems totally preposterous. Indeed, this is quite the wrong way of looking at the question.

It is important not to lose sight of the fact that the reason for building any form of competence at all into machines is so that the machine might better serve its user. In this sense, an intentional machine is one that takes into account its user's intentionality while retaining a knowledge of its own 'machineness'. For example, if the user were to mention the word bacon a properly attuned intentional machine would enter into a discussion with the user about what *his* experience of bacon might be. At the same time it would gently remind the user that it, the machine, had no real experience of it, but was prepared to accept that the user's experience was valid and worth storing.

As part of this process there comes the inevitable point at which the machine must, as part of its knowledge, contain a theory of the way in which its human user might acquire knowledge. It is at this precise point that the inadequacy of knowledge-acquisition schemes in current expert systems becomes more than apparent. Logical databases and logical programs do not at present approach a representation for an expert's statement of the form 'I know X' or 'I believe X' or even the more mischievous, 'I like X'.

It is for this reason that much attention in what follows will be given to theories of human acquisition of behaviour. Centrally, consideration will be given to a theory of the acquisition of personality: the *personal construct theory*. This has been discussed briefly in Chapter 1, where repertory grids were introduced. Here it will be considered in much greater depth, in order to see whether it holds hope for the foundation of design principles for intentional machines. Not only does such a theory need to be scrutinized, but also a brief review of the theoretical basis of the current expert system/artificial intelligence paradigm is necessary.

Controversies in artificial intelligence

There are two major controversies that are likely to apply evolutionary pressure to the artificial intelligence paradigm. The first centres on whether the algorithmic models discussed in Chapter 4, when taken together, form a theory of human intelligence. Indeed, Margaret Boden in her most distinguished book, *Artificial Intelligence and Natural Man* (1977), defines the field as, '... research that is somehow relevant to human knowledge and psychology ...'. At the same time, equally influential texts such as that by Niels Nilsson, *Principles of Artificial Intelligence* (1980), see an algorithmic theory still very much as a goal rather than an achievement of artificial intelligence and values the algorithms mainly as products of good engineering that take computers into the solution of difficult computing tasks.

The second controversy rages around the question of machine intentionality. This focuses mainly on language-understanding programs where devotees of the artificial intelligence paradigm, or believers in 'strong' artificial intelligence, claim that story-understanding algorithms provide a theory of understanding. Philosopher John Searle is the major opponent of this belief as he sees object relatedness as a central facet of any system for which it can be claimed that 'understanding' is one of its properties.

It is proposed here to subject the first of these controversies to what has been learnt in Chapter 3 about the nature of modern theory, and then to ask what sort of theoretical approach needs to be adopted in order to encompass intentionality as one of its theorems.

THE APPROPRIATENESS OF THEORIES IN INTELLIGENT SYSTEMS

It was seen in Chapter 3 that, as a result of the demise of Euclidean thinking in mathematics, theory is seen as being related to mechanisms in the world by a hypothesis. The theories themselves may be totally valid, purely on the basis of their self-consistency. The fact that axioms are triggered by real systems and theorems are predictive of behaviour in such systems simply points to the validity of the hypothesis, and not to the validity of the theory which must be verified by mathematical and logical means. A diagram of the difference in what may be called pre-Hilbertian and post-Hilbertian mathematical thinking is shown in Figure 7.1(a) and (b). This sees Hilbert as the watershed between Euclidean and non-Euclidean mathematics, as he was the first to suggest that axioms may be triggered by any ideas in the real world and not only geometrical ones. This point is vital if there is ever going to be a theory that relates to human behaviour.

Looking at artificial intelligence programming styles, a theory appears to consist of structural axioms (such as model states related by production rules) and behavioural theorems, ie the performance of the system at run time. This is illustrated in Figure 7.1(c). A good example of this are the programs written by James Meehan. The input to such programs are fact-like data about the elements of a story, and production rules that enable the program to make arbitrary but constrained transitions between story states. At run time, these state sequences are output and ostensibly have a story-like nature.

Does this seeming success have anything to say about the psychology of human story telling? Some might argue that the story is an emergent theorem from the given axioms. This very statement may be criticized on the grounds that the entire structure of the programs (axioms) was stacked so as to achieve the theorem, which falls short of the rigour that one would expect in a mathematical situation. However, this criticism could be put aside, only to reveal the more difficult

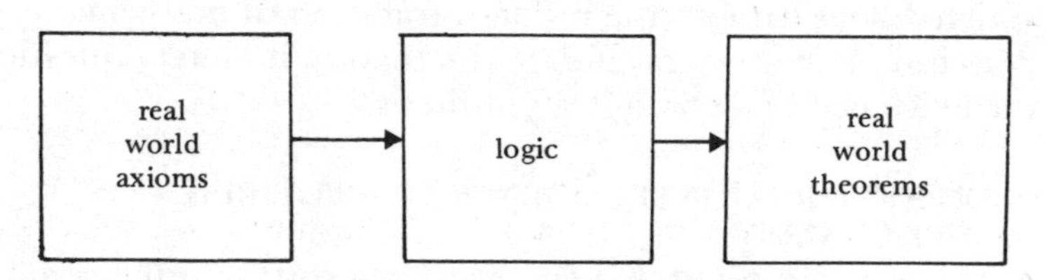

(a) pre-Hilbertian theory

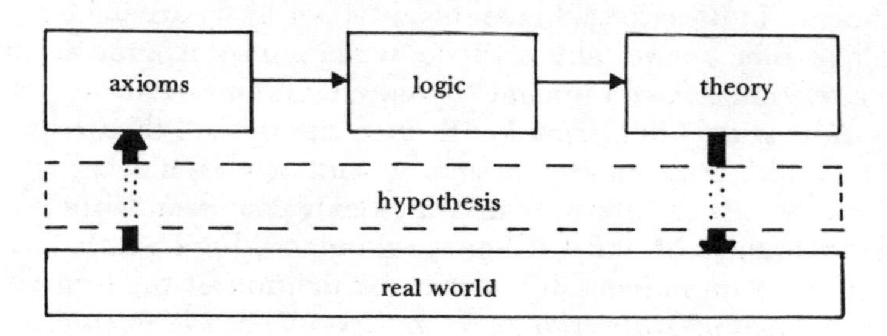

(b) post-Hilbertian theory

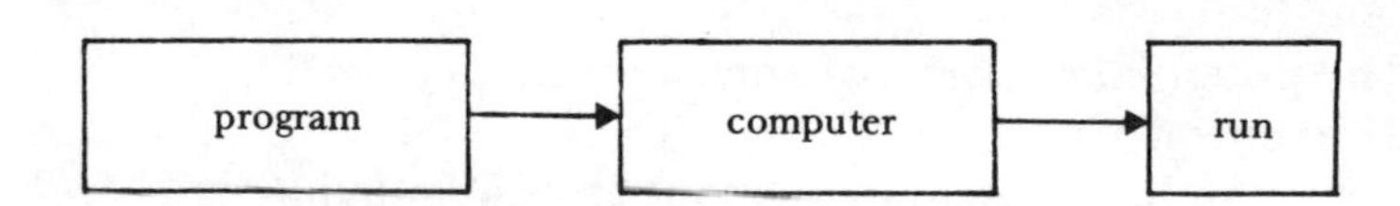

(c) artificial intelligence

Figure 7.1. *Theories of intelligent systems and the real world*

question of whether the successful computer run really justifies the statement that the program is *about* human story telling.

Unfortunately there is no evidence, not even a hypothesis, that links the programs or axioms of the theory to human activity. This, true to the modern tradition of mathematics, does not in any way invalidate the theory, it merely questions the existence of an 'about' hypothesis.

FROM ARTIFICIAL INTELLIGENCE TO ARTIFICIAL INTENTIONALITY

It has been suggested that the paradigm shift in intelligent systems is likely to be driven by the lack of intentionality within current artificial intelligence programming styles. It has also been said that aiming to build intentional machines may be a futile quest, while machines that take their user's intentionality into account would be at the centre of the new paradigm. In order to achieve this, it is necessary to make explicit some computable scheme, which, in itself, models the intentionality of humans, perhaps as an emergent property. Only when armed with such theory will the design of the 'new paradigm intentional system' be possible.

Theories about intentionality are being discussed within the community of philosophers, and indeed, John Searle has contributed monumentally to the clarification of the term itself in his book *Intentionality: an Essay in the Philosophy of Mind* (1984). But this is not sufficiently appealing to the mathematician as yet, to underpin the design of an intelligent system.

Amongst the alternatives, a theory in psychology that has been studied for its potential in intelligent systems is Kelly's personal construct theory.

The potential of personal construct theory (PCT)

The central aim of the theory is to explain those characteristics in human beings that are personal to the individual. Therefore, in psychology, PCT comes under the heading of a theory of personality. In reality, PCT has both its followers and its dissidents. Amongst its followers there are many clinical psychologists and industrial practitioners who use the theory as a means for assessing people's views of themselves and the objects or people around them. Essentially the theory is used to make explicit feelings and processes that may not be immediately available in conscious explanations. The dissidents tend to be sceptical of the measurement techniques that are derived from the theory. On the whole, however, PCT is now seen as one among several theories of personality.

Kelly was concerned with precision. His theory is stated as one fundamental postulate and eleven corollaries. The crux of the theory is that man builds up his informational structures as a result of a basic need to predict and control the world around him. In Kelly's words, often echoed by his followers, PCT sees man as a scientist, creating and refining his hypotheses so as to be better predictive of his environment. Even if this does not directly explain intentionality in theoretical terms, it must deal with it implicitly. It is impossible to imagine man-the-scientist without a proper object relatedness within his informational structures.

The main difficulty with PCT is that as a theory, it belongs to the class of psychological theories that lacks the precision and rigour of mathematical or algorithmic theories. This process of making it rigorous is the subject of much current research. Here only the first emerging thoughts on the way in which the psychological theory may be used to provide an algorithmic theory, are presented. This will be done on the basis of looking first at the fundamental postulate and then at its eleven corollaries.

A mechanistic interpretation of PCT

THE FUNDAMENTAL AXIOM

This is stated by Kelly as: 'A person's processes are psychologically channelized by ways in which he anticipates events.' In trying to define an algorithm to encompass PCT, it becomes important to state as clearly as possible what each of the words in Kelly's formulation might mean. Therefore, what *processes* are to a person must be what the algorithm itself is to a computer. By using the word *psychologically,* the range of activities implied by the axiom is restricted to those aspects of a person that involve communication, thought and action. This may be contrasted with, say, digestion and growth. In what here shall be called the *K-algorithm* (K for Kelly), this translates rather obviously to the inclusion of internal and external informational transactions. The word *channelized* interestingly implies a state structure of some kind. Therefore in the K-algorithm it may be interpreted as just that – a state structure that relates input to output.

The word *ways,* although seemingly innocuous, being in the plural discloses Kelly's determination that explanations of the channelization process should be seen as being non-deterministic. This means that one state and an input condition may lead to several states. As an aside, there is a theorem in automata theory that states that any non-deterministic state structure can always be represented by a deterministic one. This means that by seeking a non-deterministic structure for the K-algorithm one has not skipped to some level of physical unreality. To make the point, it is possible to use an example.

Consider an automaton that has states: 'hungry', 'eat cake', 'eat apple', 'get fat' and 'be healthy'. A non-deterministic way of arranging these states may be as shown in Figure 7.2.

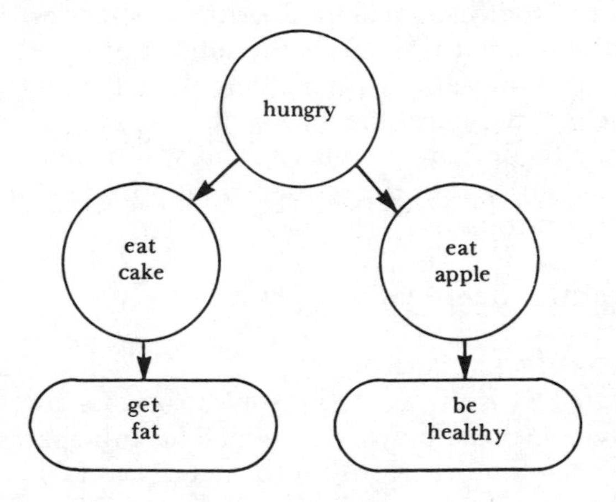

Figure 7.2. *A non-deterministic automaton*

In the current context, this may be interpreted as saying that there are two *ways* in which the automaton may move on from the hungry state. This is a perfectly proper way of representing a mechanism. It has been used before, particularly in the parts of this book that deal with the mathematics of language and algorithms for artificial intelligence. The only problem with this is that the same task needs recasting so that it is represented by a diagram with only one exit per state. This assures that the system may be implemented by techniques discussed in Chapter 2. A simple way of doing this is shown in Figure 7.3.

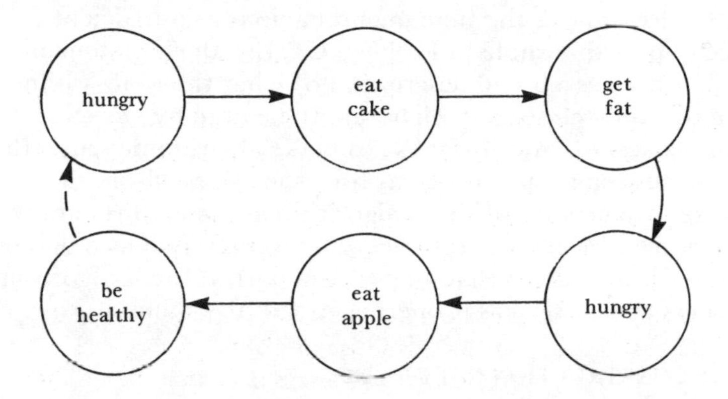

Figure 7.3. *A deterministic version of Figure 7.2*

Clearly Figure 7.3, even intuitively, has more of a feel of a thought process than Figure 7.2, even though the two express the same concepts.

Returning to the fundamental axiom, the word *anticipates* points to the fact that the main built-in criterion in the system is that of being able to anticipate its own input. The way in which the axiom is worded suggests that the overriding force in the development of the channelizing itself (ie the creation of the state structure in a learning automaton) is the success or failure of the anticipation.

The word *event* also refers to a mental state that is related to the realities of the world. Again, a study of Kelly's writing has revealed that the word *event* has a certain complexity due to a possible ambiguity as to whether it represents some facet of the physical aspects of the world or the mental object to which they relate. Current thinking has it that it must be the latter. Thus, Kelly too has something to say about intentionality, and it is a challenging notion that, since object relatedness seems to be engrained in PCT, an algorithmic version of the theory is likely to clarify many of the issues surrounding the idea of machine intentionality.

In the light of this it may be possible to specify a little

more closely what the K-algorithm embraces. This can be done by restating the fundamental axiom in algorithmic terminology: 'The K-algorithm is *about* human thought and action. Its state structure is developed by optimizing the excellence with which it anticipates external events.'

Clearly, just as the fundamental axiom is insufficient to encompass the whole of Kelly's PCT, the above statement only provides a broad description of what the K-algorithm is about. Kelly chooses to elaborate the axiom by eleven corollaries. In order for these to make algorithmic sense, they must be seen as specifications for procedures within the overall framework of the K-algorithm as stated. From now on, some of Kelly's corollaries will be translated into descriptions of procedures that might form part of the K-algorithm. Others will be seen as properties of the algorithm.

THE CONSTRUCTION COROLLARY

> 'A person anticipates events by construing their replications.'

Kelly used the word *construing* to mean 'placing an interpretation'. The crux of this corollary is the word *replications.* Here the meaning of an internal representation becomes a little clearer. The meaningful aspects of real-world events that qualify as internal representations of an event-like nature are the replicative aspects of the world itself. For example, the word 'night' has the peak of its meaning in the fact that it is noticeable through its replicative occurrence every 24 hours, with darkness being the main feature of the replication. In other words, if a visitor from another, perpetually lit world, in which darkness may be achieved only by crawling into a cave, were to visit Earth for only 24 hours, he would not develop a concept for night. He would remain only with the concept of darkness and would not be able to anticipate it as a function of time. In other words, any interpretation that is placed on night derives from its replication in time. Clearly, the replication of things does not only refer to things that repeat themselves in time. Space, or just association, could have replicative properties. For example, people recur in space and allow us to place an interpretation on their existence. Abstractions such as 'honours degrees' are associated in the UK with the replicative concept of a university, and therefore assume a replicative nature of their own.

The construction corollary requires the following *construction procedure* in the K-algorithm: 'The procedure assigns labels to replicative features in the input data stream.' Clearly, there is much detail missing in this specification as to exactly how a system might be designed to extract such features. This may, for the purpose of the current argument, be seen as a matter of technical elaboration.

THE INDIVIDUALITY COROLLARY

> 'Persons differ from each other in their construction of events.'

This was Kelly's way of stressing the personal nature of his proposed mechanism, an individual's right to his own individuality. He also showed his disapproval of theories in psychology which classify large numbers of people under the same psychological banner. For example, theories of learning developed during the 1940s and 1950s arose from the psychological paradigm of behaviourism, where the learning behaviour of humans was equated to the bar-pressing performance of rats under reward-punishment conditions. In a technical sense, this corollary merely draws attention to the fact that the state structures created through the construction procedure will be individual to each mechanism, depending on the individual nature of the input data stream. This implies that the state structure cannot rely on some pre-programmed knowledge that merely becomes enabled by the input data stream. It leads to the following technical version of the individuality corollary.

The *individuality of the K-algorithm state structure* is as follows: 'The construction procedure is such that it builds an operative state structure only on the basis of the input data stream, leading to state structures that are individual to mechanisms exposed to individual data streams. The pre-programming needs only to provide some control for this procedure.'

THE DICHOTOMY COROLLARY

> 'A person's construction system is composed of a finite number of dichotomous constructs.'

This corollary is central both to the way in which Kelly structured his theory, and the nature of the atoms of the

K-algorithm. Kelly argued that an interpretation cannot be placed on an event by a single statement. If I were to say that 'Peter is good' this would leave my feeling open to further interpretation. I could be saying that he was good as opposed to clumsy in the context of a skill or good as opposed to naughty. Therefore, although the attribute 'good' has been used twice, the total concept used for placing an interpretation was 'good-clumsy' or 'good-naughty', two totally different frameworks.

Such two-pole frameworks are the atoms of Kelly's theory, as indeed they must be in the K-algorithm. Thus a construct is an atomic function that takes an event as input data, and returns a value which is one of the two poles of the construct.

The *dichotomy function* is as follows: 'The K-algorithm is largely composed of a finite number of atomic functions. These are called construct functions and are used for the purpose of placing interpretations on events. Each such function uses an event as an argument and returns one of two attributes. The function is fully defined by these two attributes.'

THE ORGANIZATION COROLLARY

> 'Each person characteristically evolves, for his convenience in anticipating events, a construction system embracing ordinal relationships between constructs.'

Here, a link is established between the dichotomous constructs of the last corollary. Not stated in the corollary itself, but clearly described in Kelly's writing, is the fact that this link can have two aspects: implication and attribution.

The implicative link may be illustrated by the pair of constructs: 'classical-pop' and 'good-bad'. In some people's minds all musical events that are classical are also good while all those that are of the pop kind are also bad. Thus, the classical-jazz construct implies the good-bad construct, and in a logical sense, the latter includes, or subsumes the former.

The attributional link, on the other hand, directs attention to a further attribute that can be used on the construct itself. Thus, in some people's mind the construct classical-jazz in itself may be seen as being a classifying construct where others may see it as being qualitative. Hence, the qualifying-classifying construct also subsumes the classical-jazz one, but in this different, attributional, sense.

Another word that is of great importance in this corollary is 'evolves'. This implies that the links described earlier are made as a part of a development process. Hence this corollary contains the learning mechanism of the system. This may be reflected in the K-algorithm in the following technical sense.

The *organization procedure* is as follows: 'The K-algorithm has an evolutionary structure. Links are made and broken according to success or otherwise in anticipating events. The links are of two kinds, and are made between the construct functions. The first kind is forged through an assessment that whenever one construct function is used to assess an element another is always used in the same way, then the link is established. The other is made, when in order to anticipate events, a construct function in itself is given an event-like relationship to its superordinate construct. Thus, the construct functions and their two types of one-directional links form a *construct database.'*

THE CHOICE COROLLARY

> 'A person chooses for himself that alternative in a dichotomized construct through which he anticipates the greater possibility for extension and definition of his system.'

In this corollary Kelly did two things: one mechanistic and the other almost philosophical. At the practical level he allocated construct poles to events and other constructs, providing a clue to the way in which he saw that this system anticipates events. For example, the event of 'going to a party' may be assigned to the 'happy' side of a 'happy-gloomy' construct, which in a broader consideration may lead the subject to anticipate that going to a party will be a happy event for him. More than this, Kelly suggested that the allocation is made in such a way that it provides greater growth for the system. This is done by linking constructs to a highly superordinate construct, 'elaborative-restrictive'. For example, 'happy-gloomy' would be linked to 'elaborative-restrictive' in that order. This would be based on the general experience that deciding that an event is likely to be happy will lead to a further exploration of it, while the other way round would lead to a less out-going outcome that would prove to be restrictive.

Philosophically, Kelly here does away with the classical need for 'motivation' or 'goal directedness' on which many philosophies of behaviour are based. In PCT, it is *curiosity* that motivates the individual, or, in Kellian terms, the need to extend and resolve ambiguities in the construction system.

Computationally, this leads to the following mechanism. The *choice procedure:* 'During the evolution of the K-algorithm, all constructs are eventually linked to an 'elaborative-restrictive' construct, according to whether the elaboration of the system is facilitated. New events are then assigned to the elaborative side of the construct, when other factors do not define the choice.'

THE RANGE COROLLARY

> 'A construct is convenient for the anticipation of a finite range of events only.'

This is a self-evident statement which points to the fact that there is a three-way relationship between any event and a construct: assigned to pole 1, assigned to pole 2, and irrelevant. It is in this way that a construct only relates to a subset of all the possible events that might be anticipated by the system.

The *range property* is as follows: 'The K-algorithm assigns finite sets of elements to each construct. Conversely, when an event is to be anticipated, the algorithm returns only those constructs which contain the element, stressing the selected pole.'

This points to a curious anomaly in the way that the word 'anticipates' is used. This is not intended to be a sort of fortune-telling exercise. The word 'anticipates' should be read as the act of construing events that are either generated by 'the environment' or are reactions to such an event arising from the process of following up the links within the construct structure.

THE EXPERIENCE COROLLARY

> 'A person's construction system varies as he successively construes the replication of events.'

This implies that the process of restructuring the system of constructs is free to be continuously updated. It is at this point that Kelly introduced the role of emotions into his theory. An emotion such as anxiety may be the speech act that describes a need for a major change in the restructuring of the construct system. It is through this that the theory becomes useful in a clinical sense. The therapist, recognizing the nature of the patient's construction system, can reveal this to the patient himself, and thus help in a patient-led process of reconstruction. Technologically, this translates to an important specification for the K-algorithm.

The *experience specification* is as follows: 'The K-algorithm must make provision for successive alterations to its construct database, optimized on its ability to anticipate events. Provision should also be made for a reporting function that keeps the user informed of the magnitude of the restructuring task so that he (the user) can take part in the restructuring process.'

This specification relates the K-algorithm to the familiar process of knowledge elicitation in expert systems, as discussed in Chapter 6.

THE MODULATION COROLLARY

> 'The variation of a person's construction system is limited by the permeability of the constructs within whose range of convenience the variants lie.'

This points to a property rather than a specification or a procedure. It also introduces a new measure that can be applied to constructs, that of *permeability*. This is merely a measure of the likely *size* of the set of events that is applicable to a particular construct. It is most important, however, that this be seen as a potential size and not an achieved size. For example, the construct 'good-bad' has high permeability as it is likely to be applicable to many events, while a construct such as 'musically talented-tone deaf' has lower permeability. The associated technical property refers to the variability of the construct database.

The *modulation property* is as follows: 'The adaptability of the construct database is dependent on itself. In particular, the K-algorithm has flexibility to adapt the construct database only within the limits of the permeability of the constructs it already contains.'

This suggests that early in the development of the construct database, the constructs need to be permeable so as to allow the system to adapt more flexibly. It also suggests that the superordinate constructs, as created by the organization procedure, are likely to be more permeable than their subordinates.

THE FRAGMENTATION COROLLARY

> 'A person may successively employ a variety of construction subsystems which are internally incompatible with each other.'

The importance of this corollary is that it draws attention to the fact that constructs may, on different occasions, be used in ways that need not be logically compatible with one another. In technical terms this implies a certain degree of context dependence. For example, a jazz enthusiast may see the construct 'good-bad' as being superordinate to the construct 'jazz-pop' (in that order), should he be anticipating his enjoyment or otherwise in listening to some music. However, were he to anticipate the event of dancing to some music he might make the link exactly the other way round, 'pop' with 'good' and 'jazz' with 'bad'. Technically, this involves a concept of addressing the construct database, with context as one of the addressing parameters.

Fragmentation through context addressing is as follows: 'The construct database may contain fragments that embody the same constructs, but link them in different ways which need not be logically compatible with one another. The selection of a particular fragment must depend on context data, and be implemented through an addressing scheme that depends on the context.'

In the above example, it would be the events 'listening' and 'dancing' that would address different fragments of the construct database.

THE COMMONALITY COROLLARY

> 'To the extent that a person employs a construction of experience which is similar to that employed by another, his processes are similar to those of another person.'

In PCT this is seen as a corollary that balances the individuality corollary, in the sense that it allows that there could be partial commonality between the construction systems of two persons. It can then be said that psychologically and only to some limited extent, the two individuals are similar. A trivial technical interpretation of this notion is that two different instantiations of the K-algorithm may turn out to be similar. However, a more interesting interpretation of this and the next corollary relates to implications for the man-machine interface.

It is expected that the only use for the K-algorithm will be in an expert system mode. The construct system will, under the guidance of its user, largely be moulded into the user's own system. As has been said at the beginning of this chapter, this is the most likely way in which the K-algorithm and its resulting construct database will be helpful to the user. Therefore, the commonality corollary suggests a *capability* for the K-algorithm.

The *commonality capability* is as follows: 'If placed under the control of a single user, the K-algorithm has the capability of building up a construct database which, within certain constraints, is given a construction of experience that makes its behaviour similar to that of its user.'

This must not be taken too literally, as the processes in the machine are second-hand and based on a reconstruction of experience provided for it by the user. It is a matter of simple program design, to keep the user reminded of the fact that it is his own experience that is being built up in the machine. It would be senseless for the machine to output a sentence such as, 'I like bacon'. The program design should be such that the commonality capability is brought out through the machine saying, 'I anticipate that *you* like bacon'.

THE SOCIALITY COROLLARY

> **'To the extent that one person construes the construction processes of another, he may play a role in the social process involving the other person.'**

The point that Kelly emphasized with this corollary is that, in order for people to establish social and cultural links, they need not *think* in the same way (have the same construction systems). It is sufficient that they should construe each other's systems. In simpler terms the corollary says that people need to understand each other, without necessarily being alike.

This assumes a great deal of importance if translated into

the technical domain, particularly with reference to the man-machine interface. It should be possible for the user and the machine to share knowledge of each other's construct system. This is a direct consequence of the way in which the construct database in the machine is derived within the K-algorithm. This leads to the final property of the algorithm which can now be formally stated as the *sociality property:* 'The construct database may be understood by the user even if it develops idiosyncrasies resulting from the construction process. Similarly, it is possible for the machine to *distinguish* its own construct database from that of its user, and report on its findings. To this extent, it is possible for a user and the machine to share in a man-machine social process.'

It is this process of *distinguishing* that will bring a machine based on a K-algorithm closer to being endowed with intentionality than machines seen so far.

Applications of intentional machines

Having gone to quite a lot of trouble to establish a path whereby an intentionally improved relationship between man and machine might be established, it is necessary to say a little of some factual ways in which such systems might be used. After all, the strength of the K-algorithm seems to lie in transferring some of the personal characteristics of the user into the machine. That, in itself, only seems to impart some of the weaknesses of humans into the machine.

The most obvious, but probably the most distant application of the K-algorithm, is its application in home computing. For example, it could form the basis of a personal advisor. There are two ways in which this could be helpful. First, the building phase of the construct database could be a 'head-clearing' exercise of a therapeutic nature. Second, it could make highly practical information available to its user: a bit like a discussion with a helpful friend. The conversation might be about going to a party where there was going to be some pop music played and you felt uncertain whether to go or not. The computer might suggest that although you generally do not enjoy pop, should the possibility of dancing arise, then this is something that you might enjoy.

Such a scheme may have even more relevance for the elderly, who may wish to be reminded of things that need to be done regularly, but may be easily forgotten. True, this can now be done with simple storage of data, but it is the close relationship between person and machine that may be afforded by the K-algorithm, which would ease the rather forbidding nature of current systems. Clearly, for these applications it would be nice to have a system such as that shown in Figure 5.4 where contact through a keyboard would not be a matter for concern for the user. Indeed, the K-algorithm would be ideal for the IKBS part of this kind of system.

Away from home computing, two major application areas become apparent, these are computer-aided management and computer-aided design. In these areas the K-algorithm would have to be interwoven with access to specialist tasks that already exist in the world of software. For example, a manager might need access to financial prediction packages based on existing programs. But it would be the K-algorithm that would act as a sort of supervisory program through which the manager would build up his relationship with the computer.

In computer-aided design in most subject domains too, the user needs to be able to access specialized data and calculation procedures. An example would clarify the role that the K-algorithm might play in this process. Say that the design domain is that of digital systems. Take two designers, each approaching the design in his own individual way. The first may prefer to look at similar designs in his database and assess them against constructs such as 'fast-slow', 'new chips-old chips', and anticipate (in Kelly's terminology) which earlier design should be looked at first. Note that the constructs mentioned are all likely to be linked to a superordinate construct of the 'good-bad' type. As a second step the designer might start modifying the selected design, choosing his techniques against an anticipation of their likely effect on the design. This process of selection would be guided by the construct database within the K-algorithm.

To stress the individual nature of what has been described above, the design style described may be contrasted to that of the second designer. He may have a more analytic turn of mind, and require that the specification be first subjected by the computer to a decomposition analysis which returns groupings of system states that remain grouped under inputs (for details of this technique, refer to partition-pair theory in textbooks on digital system design). It is notoriously difficult for a computer to make sensible decisions about how these groupings may be combined to arrive at a good design. It is here that the designer may call on a K-algorithm anticipation of which groupings are better than others. This might be done on totally non-rigorous grounds through constructs such as 'neat-messy', 'familiar-unknown', etc. These, again, link to a superordinate construct, 'desirable-not desirable'.

It is interesting that the two designers could come up with exactly the same design. Further, it is also worth noting here that the knowledge database (facts and calculations, stored solutions and theoretical formulae) would be identical in the two cases. Indeed, the two systems are identical to start with, but, both being endowed with the K-algorithm, will develop totally different control structures, highly tailored to the needs of the designer.

Summary

There are areas of computing in artificial intelligence where there is considerable room for improvement. This improvement has been laid at the feet of 'intentionality'. In fact, this term has been given a meaning that encompasses the lack of understanding that current computing schemes display. It is hardly surprising therefore that this is where improvements are likely to be made.

Personal construct theory has been presented as one way of generating an algorithm which allows an artificial system to absorb the work style of its user. It has been argued in the final section of this chapter that such a system could make knowledge-based systems much more available in areas that are in some way less defined and less mechanical than those discussed in earlier chapters. But personal construct theory is not the only approach to this problem. The field is wide open and this chapter merely acts as a pointer to much exciting research that still needs to be done.

POSTSCRIPT

The foundations of a paradigm?

Casting a glance over the earlier chapters of this book reveals that rather a large number of topics have been introduced as forming the basis of a science of intelligent system design. The aim here is to integrate some of these strands by attempting to show how they relate to one another. It may be helpful therefore to identify the salient characteristics of an ideal intelligent system.

It is most likely that part of such a system will contain the classical memory/central processor structure which has been the basis of computer design since it was first proposed by John Von Neumann in 1947. But it is also likely that other parts will have more specialized structures of a parallel kind: the schemes described for image processing and pattern recognition in Chapter 5 are examples. But most important of all, the specialized computing language will have become part of the internal engineering of the system. Interaction with the user should take place in natural language, preferably through speech and images and avoiding, as far as possible, the use of keyboards.

Right from the start, in Chapter 1, it has been argued that an intelligent system would have to do more than merely store knowledge and rules and regurgitate the results in a superficial imitation of human intelligence. It was made clear that the true aim of an intelligent system of the future should be the ability to build up a fund of general knowledge (as opposed to special knowledge as is the case in current expert systems) which would enable it to 'understand' its user while at the same time keeping the user aware of its own limitations as a machine. From a standpoint of the limited achievements of current technology in this direction, this seems an awfully long haul, fraught with problems without immediate solutions. So, while this book cannot reveal such solutions, its aim has been to describe those areas of technical and theoretical expertise within which the answers are likely to be found.

The first direction in which to look was indicated by the fact that *memory* is at the heart of any knowledge-acquisition system. Mathematically such systems are described within a field known as *automata theory.* Chapter 2 served to provide an introduction to the fundamentals of a branch of automata theory, that of *finite-state machines.* A central property of this theory is that it enables a designer to describe the internal behaviour of an information-handling machine in abstract terms, without reference to hardware or software. In fact, it was shown in Chapter 2 that designs expressed in the language of automata theory may be implemented equally well either in hardware *or* software. It was also shown that such automata provide the designer with a modelling tool in topics as wide ranging as card playing and dreaming. Therefore, finite-state automata provide tools for the designer not so much of a problem-solving nature but more as a precise way of expressing models and designs.

The words *finite state* in fact imply finite memory. Chapter 3 demonstrated that this fact alone makes finite-state automata synonymous with an algebraic system known as a semi-group. In order to provide a better insight into the significance of this fact a background to such algebraic systems has been provided. Finite-state machines are inadequate for those informational structures that occur in language-like systems. Thus, in Chapter 3 the step was taken to find models beyond semi-groups. These were mainly the mathematical linguistic structures described by Chomsky and the universal automata of Turing. It seems clear that the mathematical foundations of the design of future intelligent systems will rest squarely in the area of abstract algebraic systems.

Where Chapter 3 was seen to give a mathematical background to intelligent system design, Chapter 4 centred on the algorithmic and computational aspects. What has recently been researched in the way in which tasks accomplished by humans may be transferred to a computer is encompassed by the field of artificial intelligence. This science is based on finding algorithms (or computing procedures) that carry out such tasks. Examples of such algorithms in game-playing and problem-solving tasks were presented to illustrate how the transfer was achieved in well-known cases. This chapter also introduced the first glimpse of artificial vision, as seen from the algorithmic point of view. Clearly, much of human intelligent behaviour is both directed towards processing vision and is aided by the presence of vision.

Unfortunately, the coldly logical algorithms such as used in game playing and problem solving, prove to be inadequate when it comes to coping with visual data. For this reason methods that employ statistical automata were introduced. It is on such methods that many current intelligent vision systems are based. Chapter 4 ended by considering another human attribute: the use of natural language. This involves algorithms that go beyond Chomsky's grammatical models through the use of set theory to encompass the meaning of simple sentences about simplified areas of discourse. These ideas were originated by Terry Winograd at the Massachusetts Institute of Technology and are now the basis on which language-understanding programs are being written.

In response to the often expressed idea that artificial intelligence programs seem not to emerge from oversimplified application areas, Chapter 5 introduced a note of realism by considering practical problems for which intelligent systems may be required in the area of automation. Here there are pressing needs for making the interaction between operator and system an ever increasingly intelligent one. Artificial vision came under scrutiny again as it is here that intelligent decisions may need to be made twenty or thirty times each second in order to keep up with the flow of parts in a manufacturing process. It is here that the need for restructuring the hardware of a conventional computing system was raised and three levels of progression, each with a higher degree of intelligence, were introduced.

Not all work in artificial intelligence could be said to operate in unrealistically oversimplified environments. Certain areas of human expertise are in themselves constrained and logical enough to form a database for a conventional system. Such schemes go under the heading of expert systems and were discussed fully in Chapter 6. Much current research is based on systems of this kind. For example, fifth-generation computing is based on the notion that with falling costs of computer memory devices, expert system schemes that are currently relegated to specialist areas such as oil prospecting or the analysis of mass spectra, could form the basis of generally intelligent systems. Chapter 6 provided an introduction to this important topic and allows the reader to assess its potential with respect to the hardware approaches described in Chapter 5.

It was with Chapter 6 that the discussion of known and tried ideas in the design of intelligent systems ended. Unfortunately, the full specification given at the beginning of this chapter for an intelligent system cannot be met solely with these techniques. Recalling that the aim was to produce systems 'with the ability to build up a fund of general knowledge which would enable them to *understand* their users, while at the same time keeping their users aware of their own limitations as machines', it is clear that the future will need to bring some added ingredients to existing methods in order to approach this aim. To this end Chapter 7 was written in a speculative vein, introducing the reader to a possible foundation for the writing of intelligent programs drawn from known theories of human personality. Although this topic is not fully researched at the moment, it may encourage the reader to think along lines that might produce what seems to be a most necessary paradigm shift in this area.

In design textbooks on other subjects, say electronic circuits, it is possible to unfold ideas from mathematics, physics and the laws of electricity in a smooth and related way, strongly directed towards designs that are well tried and tested. This is not possible in designing intelligent systems. The end products are certainly not well tried and tested and the systems themselves are open to definition. But this is what makes the subject an absorbing one. The opportunities open to the reader are vast. Rapidly advancing computer technology is his ally. This book therefore has sought to highlight those principles that are likely to remain unchanging in this turbulently progressing field. It has also presented current thinking on systems designed to date. The real advances in intelligent system design are only limited by the imagination of designers in the future.

Bibliography

Chapter 1

Bannister, D.; Fransella, F. (1971) *Inquiring Man* Penguin, Harmondsworth, UK.
A good introduction to personal construct theory and grids

Chomsky, N. (1957) *Syntactic Structures* Mouton, France.
This is the classical work on mathematical models of grammar

Dennett, D. (1978) *Brainstorms* Harvester Press, Hassocks, UK.
Contains the attribution argument about intentionality

Kelly, G. (1955) *A Theory of Personality* Norton, New York, USA.
The classical description of personal construct theory

Searle, J. Minds, brains and programs. *Behavioural and Brain Sciences* 1980, 2, 417-424.
The paper that refutes computer understanding using the Chinese Room example

Shannon, C.E. A symbolic analysis of relay and switching circuits. *Trans. AIEE* 1938, 57, 713-722.
The paper in which switching circuits were related to logic for the first time

Von Bertalanffy, L. (1973) *General System Theory* Penguin, Harmondsworth, UK.
An attempt to unify systems under one theory

Weizenbaum, J. ELIZA: A computer program for the study of natural language and communication between man and machine. *Comm. ACM* 1966, 9, 36-45.

Chapter 2

Aleksander, I. (1978) *The Human Machine* Georgi Publications, St Saphorin, Switzerland.
Describes applications of automata theory in the life sciences

Aleksander, I.; Hanna, F.K. (1978) *Automata Theory: An Engineering Approach* Edward Arnold, London, UK.
Provides a good, detailed account of automata theory

Chapter 3

Aleksander, I.; Hanna, F.K. (1978) *see details listed earlier*

Hersch, R.; Davies, P.J. (1983) *The Mathematical Experience* Penguin-Pelican, Harmondsworth, UK.
An excellent introduction to modern mathematics for the uninitiated

Meschkowski, H. (1968) *Introduction to Modern Mathematics* Harrap, London, UK.
A little more taxing than the previously mentioned text

Chapter 4

Aleksander, I.; Burnett, P. (1983) *Reinventing Man: The Robot Becomes Reality* Kogan Page, London, UK.
An introduction to artificial intelligence for the uninitiated

Boden, M. (1977) *Artificial Intelligence and Natural Man* Harvester Press, Hassocks, UK.
A classical text seen from the point of view of psychology

Nilsson, N.J. (1980) *Principles of Artificial Intelligence* Tioga, Palo Alto, USA.
A comprehensive description of engineering aspects

Chapter 5

Aleksander, I. (ed.) (1983) *Artificial Vision for Robots* Kogan Page, London, UK.
A collection of papers on practical pattern recognition

Aleksander, I.; Burnett, P. (1983) *see details listed earlier*
This contains a simple introduction to the WISARD system

Boden, M. (1977) *see details listed earlier*
Provides a lucid description of artificial vision in artificial intelligence

Coiffet, P; Chirouze, M. (1983) *An Introduction to Robot Technology* Kogan Page, London, UK.
A good introduction to the intricacies of robots

Duff, M.J.B. (1983) *Computing Structures for Image Processing* Academic Press, London, UK.
A collection of papers that includes descriptions of array processors

Engelberger, J. (1980) *Robotics in Practice* Kogan Page, London, UK.
A classical text taking a practical approach to robots in manufacturing industries

Chapter 6

Clark, K.L.; McCabe, F.G. (1983) *Micro-PROLOG* Prentice Hall International, London, UK.
A good introduction to PROLOG, particularly for those interested in personal computers

Mamdani, E.H. Application of fuzzy algorithms for control of simple dynamic plant. *Proc.IEE* 1974, **121** (12), 1585-1588.

Michie, D. (1979) *Expert Systems in the Microelectronic Age* Edinburgh University Press, Edinburgh, UK.
Contains papers on the earlier expert systems

Michie, D. (1980) Expert systems. *Computer Journal* 1980, **23**, 369-376.
A good introductory paper on the subject

Zadeh, L. (1979) A theory of approximate reasoning. In: *Machine Intelligence* 9th edn, Ellis Harwood, Chichester, UK.

Chapter 7

Boden, M. (1977) *see details listed earlier*

Kelly, G. (1955) *see details listed earlier*

Kuhn, T.S. (1970) *The Structure of Scientific Revolutions* University of Chicago Press, Chicago, USA.

Nilsson, N.J. (1980) *see details listed earlier*

Searle, J. (1984) *Intentionality: Essays in the Philosophy of Mind* Cambridge University Press, Cambridge, UK.

Index